TEMPTED BY THE QUEEN

THE MURDOCH MAFIA SERIES
BOOK 4

SAMANTHA BARRETT

My brother,
How you drive me nuts, make me want to commit murder
but love you all at the same time.
This one is for you, I thought it fitting since you are the
biggest drama queen.
I love you Maymond.

Authors Note

This book may make some uncomfortable with the content.
I have always sworn if I ever wrote a Mafia book, I would go
dark,
in order to stay true to my characters that is what I have
done.
Some scenes and descriptions may make you uneasy,
make you feel squeamish but rest assured there is an HEA.
For those who have read my PNR and thought they were
dark, well this is worse, so much worse but in the best way
possible.

Welcome to the Murdoch Mafia and all their fucked-up
shit.

Chapter One

Carlina

I quietly shut the door behind myself, trying to make as little noise as possible. My brothers are all light sleepers and wake at the sound of a creaking floorboard. A sigh of relief escapes me when I don't hear thundering footsteps behind me when the door clicks shut. I carry my suitcase by the handle so the sound of the rolling wheels doesn't wake them. I've made sure to time my escape well, I have a three-minute window before the new guards take over. I quicken my pace and rush to the end of the drive and slip out the side gate to meet my waiting Uber.

I don't waste time, shoving my bag on the back seat and quickly rushing around to the other side to climb in. I know they will see me on the cameras but at least by the time they figure it out, I'll be on a plane and long gone by then. They could have Luka track me but I know Bishop won't as the guilt of him knowing what happened to me at the hands of our father will still his hand.

Each of my brothers may be named after pieces of a game but I wasn't. My father could have named me queen but chose not to. In this world we live in a woman is a means to an end—someone to cook, clean and give you a son. My whole life I have been kept a secret. No one outside of my family even knows I exist, well except for Kiara and now Gage.

I know me taking off at this time is shitty as we are in the middle of a war with the other families, but I can't do it anymore.

I won't be trapped in an ivory tower waiting for someone to come and rescue me. Since being back with Kiara, her strength has rubbed off on me and shown me that I don't need a man to save me, or my brothers to protect me. I need to fight my own battles and make my own mistakes without Bishop or King bailing me out. The twins and I are close, Rook and I more so. I know me not telling him I'm leaving is going to hurt him but I need to do this for me. I have to get away from this place and clear my head. I need to heal away from my family and that fucking house of pain. Nightmares plague me every night I'm in that house. Every night I close my eyes, I'm plagued by my past and things that were done to me as a child.

***

I thought passing through security at the airport I would get flagged because of my last name, but I didn't. The law may know what my family does but they can't prove a fucking thing. Bishop never flies commercial for this reason.

I find my seat and quickly place my purse under the seat in front of me. It may sound shallow but I feel giddy over the fact I'm flying economy and not first class, or on a private jet. This is something normal people would do and I love the fact I get to be one of them, even if it is for a short time.

I rest my head back and close my eyes, allowing myself to soak in this moment. I've never been anywhere on my own. I have always had a guard, my brother or one of our maids escort me whenever I left the house. It used to piss me off growing up. If someone recognized my brothers, they had to say I was their date for the night so they didn't know I was Tony Murdoch's bargaining chip until I was of *age*. I scoff at the thought. The bastard never gave a shit about my age while he was defiling my body nightly! Disgust rolls through me as I think about the horrible things he did to me and made me do. I was a child and my own father used my innocence against me.

I don't bother to open my eyes when I feel someone claim the seat beside me. I don't even bother to open them when the captain speaks over the intercom system or when they do the safety demonstration. All I care about is getting to Brazil and spending some time there sightseeing, then making my way to Chile. For the first time in my life, I am going to be free and it is an exhilarating feeling. When the plane takes off, I finally open my eyes and peer out the small window smiling. I say a silent goodbye to New York and hope to not be back in this place for long, *long* time. That city holds too many dark memories for me—memories I have spent most of my life trying to run from.

"It's a beautiful view, isn't it?" The husky tone of my

companion's voice washes over me, deep and manly. I close my eyes again and pray the sexy voice belongs to some hot stranger that I wouldn't mind staring at and maybe even flirting with for the next few hours. I slowly turn my gaze from the window to look at him and stifle the moan that wants to break free.

This guy is gorgeous!

His brown eyes shine with bold curiosity. The way he stares at me like he has a right is unnerving and thrilling. He shakes his head to flick the strands of his brown hair from his face, shaved on the sides and longer on the top. I run my gaze over him and pinch my mouth to the side when I see his knees are pressed firmly against the seat in front of him. He is already taller than me sitting down, which means he would dwarf my small five-foot six frame standing. His light-blue jeans with tears in the knees hug his thick thighs, his plain black cotton shirt molded to his torso like a second skin enhancing the muscles that lay beneath. I slowly pull my gaze back to his face, the five o'clock shadow that dusts his face only adds to his appeal. He smirks knowing I was just checking him out. His espresso-colored eyes darken when I dart my tongue out to moisten my lips.

"I... Uh, what was the question?" I flush when a throaty chuckle comes from him. God, this guy is beautiful. When his eyes widen, I clamp a hand over my mouth in horror. "I just said that out loud, didn't I?" I mumble from behind my hand. This time when he laughs, he doesn't hold back, it's a deep and infectious. I feel it inside my soul and envy the carefreeness about him. It's amazing to me how he can laugh so freely and not worry that the sound of his boisterous laughter is drawing the attention of the other passengers.

"Well, at least I'm not the only one sitting here thinking

how beautiful the person sitting next to me is." I roll my lips over my teeth to keep my smile from breaking free. I nod, unsure of what else to do, then begin to nibble on my bottom lip. In a bold and slightly daring move he reaches across cupping my chin and uses his thumb to free my lip. I stare at him wide-eyed and taken back that he touched me—is touching me! Whatever he sees in my eyes has him pulling back and dropping his hand into his lap. "Sorry, I... shouldn't have done that."

I shake my head to clear my wayward thoughts then clear my throat. "It's okay." I smile not wanting to make this awkward for us, we're stuck beside each other for the next nine hours. He smiles and holds out his hand. I eye it before quirking a questioning brow at him.

"My name is Vin." I smile placing my much smaller hand in his and shake it.

"Carlina." His mouth forms an O shape, making me feel slightly worried. Does he not like my name?

"What a beautiful name for a beautiful woman." I feel the blush heat my cheeks before I duck my gaze back out the window. This guy is so good for my ego. As the hours go by, Vin and I converse nonstop. He tells me he is taking a trip to just get away from work. I lie and tell him I'm visiting friends whilst on a gap year from college. Truth is, I don't plan to go to college. I don't think anyone in my family has gone to college, it wasn't an option for us. But now, thanks to Bishop, it is an option for me and the twins. I don't even know if I want to go. It would be great to live out the dorm life and party on Greek row, but it wouldn't be the same as other kids. The twins would have to be with me or I would have a shadow all the time. I wouldn't be allowed to go certain places in case it was overcrowded and made it easy for my brother's enemies to take me.

"What's wrong? The smile just dropped from your face and your eyes glazed over." I stare at Vin slightly stunned. He's known me for a few hours and already he is able to read me. My brothers can't even do that. The only person who was able to read me like a book is Kiara. I love her to death but the fact that her and Bish are together makes things hard. Her loyalty would always be to my brother. Even Rook, I know he loves me but I also know he reports everything back to Bishop. I wish I had someone of my own to care for me alone and always have my back. To the outside world my family are hotel and club owners, rich and wealthy. People try to use me to snag one of my brothers for their meal tickets. I don't even have any real fucking friends. I'm pathetic!

"Sorry, I was just thinking about my brothers and... yeah." My shoulders droop slightly on an exhale. I know they will all be up now and searching for me. I thought I would be riddled with guilt, but I'm not.

"Don't think about them then. Think of all the fun you are going to have with your friends in Brazil. Block them out and enjoy your gap year, you can deal with all that crap when you get home." I smile thankfully, he has no idea what his kind words mean to me. Vin is right, the problems back home will always be there, I need to focus on me right now.

Chapter Two

Carlina

As the plane slowly crawls along the runway to head to our gate so we can disembark, sadness washes over me. I felt at ease and more like myself than I ever have talking with Vin. Having to say goodbye to him is going to suck. As the plane comes to a stop and we wait for the fasten seatbelt to be turned off, Vin turns to me and asks,

"Where are you staying?" I may like the guy but I'm not stupid enough to name my hotel.

"Sao Paulo, for a couple weeks then I'm off to Rio for a bit." He nods and scratches at the stubble that coats his chin nodding.

"I'm in town for a bit as well. Hopefully I'll get to see

you around." I nod but then decide to take a risk and actually speak what's on my mind.

"I'd like that." His eyes darken and a sexy smirk graces his beautiful, tanned face. God, this guy is like a mix between *Henry Cavil* and *Michele Morrone*. The captain flicks the sign off and everyone stands wanting to rush off the plane to clear customs quickly. Vin steps out into the isle and motions for me to hop in front of him. I smile my thanks, grateful to be able to stretch my legs. I peek over my shoulder and try to hide my shock—he could easily fold over me, he is that freaking tall! I quickly pull my gaze back to the front in case I do something embarrassing like fawn all over him because tall guys have always made me hot and needy.

We begin to move down the aisle at a snail's pace. Every time we pause to let someone out of their seats, I feel him at my back. His body heat soaks into me, it's like an electrical current surging between us. An elderly lady climbs out in front of me and swings her purse onto her shoulder knocking me in the chest. I stumble back a step, gasping when I feel Vin's large hands gripping my waist. His hands are that big he can nearly wrap them around me. The feeling of his hands on my body short circuits my brain, my body urging me to lean into him. A throat clearing has me quickly pulling out of his hold and moving forward, I don't dare look back to gauge his reaction. I'm beyond embarrassed. I've been on my own for mere hours and here I am, fawning over the first man who is nice to me.

Get a freaking grip on yourself, Carlina!

After exiting the plane, I head straight through security and don't wait around for Vin. I need to get my bag and get the hell out of here. Which is exactly what I do. I grab my bag from baggage claim and head for the exit, not daring to look around in case I spot the bronzed God. I make my way outside to the taxi stand. The humidity here is killer, it's so thick it makes it almost hard to breathe. I join the line and when I'm the next in the queue, I feel him behind me. I don't know how but I just know it's him from the way my body heats and the hairs on the back of my neck stand up, as if warning that we are in the presence of a predator.

"Not gonna say goodbye?" I take a deep breath, square my shoulders and give myself a mental pep talk. I am Carlina Murdoch, heiress to the Murdoch Mafia. I bow to no man. I turn slowly, allowing my gaze to run from the tips of his boots all the way to his brown eyes that are now covered behind a pair of sunglasses. I keep a mask of indifference plastered across my face. I came here to escape the men in my life, not to get attached to someone on my first freaking day of freedom.

"It was lovely to meet you—"

"Come to a party with me tonight." I falter for a moment but only because he has shocked me with his forwardness.

"I've seen *Taken*. My deadbeat father may not be *Liam Neeson* but my brothers sure are." I may not be able to see his eyes, but I can tell from the way his body slightly stiffens and his brows pull in that he didn't like what I just said. I don't care, the cab pulls up and I hand my bag off to the driver, climb into the back and attempt to close the door, but he grabs hold and stops it. I scowl up at him in warning.

"Don't write me off just yet, *Gucci*. I may surprise you." I roll my eyes and slam the door closed when he releases it. The gall of him to stand there and judge me. He may think calling me Gucci is an insult but to a girl like me, it's seen more like a compliment seeing as he could have called me Walmart or Piggly Wiggly.

After finally settling into my hotel room, I decide to order some room service and chill in my room, then spend the next day exploring this beautiful city. I honestly just want to find a small café on the corner and people watch all day. It sounds stupid but I like picturing how others' lives differ from mine and envy them from afar. I love my brothers and would commit murder for them but they don't understand. They don't see the struggles I face daily just to get out of bed and put on a face so others don't see I am dying inside. Every fucking day I feel used and tainted because of the past. I've never allowed a man to touch me because all I can picture is Tony's fucking disgusting face above me grunting out his release. Just the thought alone has me racing to the bathroom and heaving over the toilet.

After ten minutes of sitting on the cold, tiled floor hunched over the porcelain bowl, I pull myself up and decide to have a shower before climbing into bed and starting fresh tomorrow. My appetite is long gone now. I won't allow thoughts of that vile pig ruin my me time. I'm under no illusions that my brothers won't track me. I have maybe a solid twenty-four hours before Luka pinpoints my exact location.

Waking the next morning to the warm sun streaming in through the sheer curtains has me smiling wide before my eyes are even open. I roll over to my back and starfish on the bed soaking up the beautiful rays of the sunlight. I slowly blink my eyes open and allow myself to bask in this moment. After five minutes of enjoying myself, I drag my ass out of bed and head for the shower so I can get ready for my day of sightseeing and being a normal teenage girl.

After showering, I decide to go with a halter neck full length maxi dress and a pair of white sandals that would match the pink of my dress. I leave my long hair out and just pin the top up to keep the long waves out of my face. I don't even bother with makeup, no one here knows me or expects anything of me. The smallest freedom of not having to wear makeup means more than anyone would ever understand.

I leave the hotel and follow my GPS to a small café in the heart of the city, it says the walk is twenty minutes but it doesn't bother me. It's an exhilarating feeling walking alone and not having men in my shadow to make sure I'm safe or doing what I have to keep my identity a secret. I sound like a brat and I don't give a shit, living like I don't exist sucked and I won't be hidden any longer.

By the time I make it to the café, I'm hot and sweaty. The weather here is killer, the humidity steals the very breath from your lungs. I smile to the beautiful waitress as she leads me toward a table out front, a small circular one right in the corner with enough shade. This is the perfect spot to people watch for hours and just be. I order a caramel latte and egg white omelet with a fruit salad. After placing my order, I slouch back in my chair and bite the bullet. I have to check in with Kiara like I promised so I pull my phone out of my purse. I cringe when I see all the missed calls and text messages from my brothers. I ignore all the messages and just as I'm about to type out a message to Kiara a shadow falls over me. I look up and my mouth drops open in shock, my phone slips through my fingers and clatters against the table.

"This seat taken, Gucci?" My brain is screaming at me to say something but no words come out. He smirks down at me before claiming the seat opposite me and motioning for the waitress. He places his order while I sit here and gawk at him. This cannot be fucking happening! "You seem surprised to see me?" That has me snapping out of my moment of stupidity, there is never a moment when I am rendered speechless, so for this man to have that effect on me isn't something I am okay with!

I lean forward and rest my forearms on the table scanning side to side to make sure no one is paying us any attention. I try to control the anger coursing through me. I have no idea why I'm angrier than I am terrified that this stranger pretty much promised to see me again and then shows up here! I should be running but nope, I'm a fool and stay here.

"How the hell did you find me?" I whisper hiss. It grates on my nerves when a self-assured smirk crosses his handsome face. Shit, no not handsome, I mean slightly good looking.

"I told you I was staying in the city, this café is around the corner from my hotel." *Oh*, I lean back in my seat trying to cover my mortification. Growing up how I did there is no such thing as a coincidence, but what he is saying is rational and may be true. When I see a look of unease and shame cross his face, I know I need to smooth this over.

"Sorry, I sounded like a right bitch, and I… I shouldn't have snapped at you." His facial expression morphs to relief and I decide here and now that this was just a coincidence after all. I mean if he was here to kill me, he could have done it dozens of times by now, right?

"Don't be, a beautiful girl like you should have her wits about her."

Chapter Three

Vincent

I can see it in her eyes, she doesn't trust me or even really believe a word that I am saying. She is smarter than I originally thought, not a dumb kid like I was led to believe. I followed her cab, she had him take the long way and then a detour before getting to her hotel. What she should have done was booked two hotels and not used her real name at the second, rookie error on her part. She crosses her arms over her chest which just serves to push her tits together and enhance my view of her cleavage. I tear my gaze from her full tits before she can catch me.

"So uh, what are you doing today?" Her candor is hesitant and unsure which tells me she isn't used to talking to strangers. I slip my mask of happiness back into place and play my part of tourist.

"No plans, just going to hang out and maybe check out some of the sights." She pushes her mouth to the side, running her gaze over me. She's trying to figure out what my angle is here, but she will never figure me out. "Did you want to join me?" Her eyes widen in surprise, her mouth opens but her reply is cut off when the waitress returns with our order. I scrunch my face in disgust when I see her food. It looks bland and tasteless but I can smell the sickly sweetness of her coffee from here. She eyes my English breakfast with hunger, her brown eyes showing her every emotion and thought. I need her to get comfortable enough with me so I can get her alone. I push my plate toward her encouraging her with a look to take what she wants.

"I have my own." The hesitancy in her tone tells me she is warring within herself over a simple plate of fucking food.

"Your plate looks fucking disgusting." She gasps and her eyes widen. "If you can look me in the eye and tell me you would rather eat yours than mine, I'll leave you be." Her eyes spark with a challenge and I wait for her to tell me to piss off and eat her own but she shocks me when she switches our plates. I stare down at the white fluffy pancake looking thing before looking at her in question.

"I'll eat yours if you eat mine." I roll my lips over my teeth to keep my crude remark from slipping free. She may be a job but even I can admit Carlina Murdoch looks like a fucking snack that I would devour. I've never been a quitter, so I grab my fork and dig in acting like this is the best fucking meal I have ever had. In truth, it's fucking disgusting and all I want to do is spit it out. I sneak a few glances at her as she eats and find myself frowning, as she smiles while she eats and does a weird little shimmy dance in her seat. I would bet she is fighting a moan from slipping free with each taste, this girl is an oddity. The fact she intrigues me tells me I need to end this, soon.

Once my plate is clean, I sit back in my chair and sip my coffee watching her eat the last piece of bacon... my fucking bacon! That bullshit she ordered didn't even fill me. I'm gonna be eating again within the hour. She places her knife and fork on top of her empty plate before leaning back in her seat with a shit eating grin on her face.

"That was amazeballs." I splutter taken off guard.

"Amaze...what?" She rolls her eyes playfully before reaching for her coffee, taking a sip and waving me off. She places her coffee back on the table and steeples her hands together eyeing me.

"So, I have plans today." I nod, not sure what else to do. "But tonight, I have no plans." I nod again which just earns me an eye roll from her. "I'm asking if you would like to do dinner... with me... tonight?" My eyes widen, surprised she would be bold enough to ask me that. The longer it takes for me to answer, her bravado slowly flees her body and her shoulders begin to sag. When her eyes drop to her lap, I reach out and place my hand a top of hers. This is the perfect opportunity to get her alone and finish this.

"I'd love to, I can pick you up about—"

"Seven would be great." I bite my tongue fighting the smile that wants to break free. She thinks she is in control here, and I'll allow her to think that, for now. She gives me her number and the name of her hotel, telling me to text her when I'm in the lobby.

After leaving Carlina at the café, I took cover on the other side of the street in a store. All she has done for the last three hours is watch people—sometimes she will smile at a couple, other times she will frown. When she frowns her nose scrunches slightly and her eyes will crinkle in the corners giving her a more youthful look. From this distance I could fool myself into thinking she is a normal teenage girl enjoying her summer break, but I do know better. She is the heiress to one of the biggest mob families in the US and her future sister-in-law's father runs the whole of Miami. What are the fucking chances Kiara Bennett would end up with Bishop, and together they will be the ultimate power couple unless they are stopped.

I push away those thoughts when Carlina stands from her chair and gathers her phone and purse. I follow after her, keeping a good distance back so she won't spot me. I keep following her until she walks inside her hotel. What she doesn't know is I have a room here as well. The room right next door to hers to be exact. I give it ten minutes before I go in and head up to my room. I quickly let myself in and lock the door behind me, then shove the chair under the handle just in case her brothers decide to show up and drag her home.

I drop onto the bed and grab my laptop, bringing up the file I have on her. Everything there is to know about Carlina Murdoch is right here. Except, after spending the time I have with her, none of this information seems accurate. She doesn't seem like the stuck-up princess she is made out to be, though she is definitely spoiled and sheltered. Finding information on this girl was a lot harder than it should have been, she is like a ghost. She wasn't even registered at school under her name, there is no birth certificate or even a fucking dental record for this girl. I read over the information again when it finally sinks in, her identity was kept secret from the world because her father didn't want anyone to know she existed.

I pull my phone from my pocket and scroll through my contacts until I land on Marco's name, he is the only person in this fucking piece of shit world I trust. Just so happens, the guy is my cousin and works in the family I fucking hate. The phone rings for so long I think he might not answer until he does.

"Vin, what can I do for ya my brother?" I smirk even though he can't see me, Marco is an informant for me. I'm in this line of work to take down each of these fucking families who think they have the right to rule over an entire fucking city and take what they want with no remorse. I've taken out men they have made deals with for years, I'm attacking their business first before going after them directly, I want them to sweat it out and know I'm coming.

"You good to talk?" I hear some shuffling in the background and a door closing before he speaks again.

"I can now, what's up?" Marco knows I'm on a job, I never discuss details of a job with him but this time I need his help. I don't kill without all the facts and I feel like I am missing something big here, I never meet the people who hire me. I'm a contractor of sorts, they contact the agency I work for—again I've never met any of them before, just came upon them by chance. The agency offers out the jobs and you can either accept or decline. Needless to say, when I saw her name I accepted the job without thought.

"You heard of Carlina Murdoch?"

"She one of the chess brother's girls?" I stifle my laughter. Marco hates the Murdoch's as much as I do. His reasons and mine differ but that's another story.

"Nah, man, apparently they have a sister." I hear his

sharp intake of breath through the phone, at least I'm not the only one who didn't know she existed.

"How the fuck do they have a sister and how the hell did we not know about her?" I fill him in on everything I know, then let him know that she is the target for this job. "If this shit is true, you take her out and you know they will come for you. Your father is in deep with the Russians right now. He and the other two families have banded together so they stand a chance against Bishop." Hearing that my piece of shit father has teamed up with rival families shocks me. That fucker never wants to split profits, so it tells me that the Murdoch's have him running scared.

"I'm not worried about them coming after me, I'll disappear for a while after this job. I need more information on this Russian shit. I need to know why the Murdoch's are making a move against the families. What has that fucker got going on with the Russians?" Marco is silent for a beat and the hairs on the back of my neck stand up.

"He and the other four families went into business with the Russians for the skin trade. We send girls, they send guns and other shit." I grip my phone so tight I fear I may shatter the fucking thing. "Ever since Bishop took over for Tony, he has been shutting it down. The other families rebelled so he is coming after everyone. He has three left to get to before he runs New York."

"He doesn't have the numbers to go after the fucking Bratva!"

"That's why he's coming after the families, he is taking over their turf and staking claim to the men to use as his army. His fiancée's father also runs Miami, so we think he'll be using Tony Bennett's men as well to take out Vlad."

Fuck, I may hate each of the families but even I can

respect what Bishop is doing here. Bishop's going to take out all the families until he is the only one left. I need to keep my fucking head on straight, finish this job and lay low until the dust settles... then go after the fucking Don of the family who sold my sister!

Chapter Four

Carlina

I text Vin twenty minutes ago to let him know I wouldn't be coming tonight, he hasn't replied. I feel bad but at the end of the day I need to keep my wits about me. Something felt off today and I've learned to trust my gut feelings. So, I ordered room service after I hopped out of the tub and now, I'm sitting here on the end of my bed watching *Supernatural* while I wait for my dinner to be delivered. My phone rings for like the hundredth time today, I glance down and when I see its Kiara, I decide to answer it.

"I'm fine." I rush to say as soon as I answer.

"Fucking hell! Bishop is losing his mind, Car. I told you to keep me updated and you haven't done that!" I can hear my brother shouting in the background and cringe. When I hear a door close I know Kiara has moved away from him. "Are you okay?" Guilt eats at me.

"I'm sorry, I should have checked in sooner but I got... distracted." By a tall, hot, bronzed God and my labia decided to think for me instead.

"Seriously? That's all you have to say after not calling or texting. I had to tell him, Car." A resigned sigh escapes me and I drop my chin to my chest.

"Is he coming to get me?" I whisper.

"No." My head snaps up in shock.

"What?"

"I told him I didn't know where you were, which isn't a lie so I never broke our deal. I told him you would check in with me, which you haven't so now he is punishing me." I gasp.

"Oh my God, is he hurting you? If he is—"

"Car!" I clamp my mouth closed and take a deep breath trying to calm down. "By punishment I mean he is using my body in the most fucking delicious way—"

"Ahhhhh, that is enough of that fucking talk!" Kiara bursts out laughing and I can't keep the smile from my own face. I'm so freaking happy her and Bish found their way to each other after all they have been through. They are made for each other.

"You sure you don't want to know about this trick your brother can do with his tongue—"

"I will fucking block you!" She laughs again. "I do not want to know what my brothers do in the privacy of their own rooms, thank you."

"Shit, he's coming!" I'm still unsure what the hell to do.

"Check in every day, Car, or I can't promise he won't come for you."

"I will." As soon as the words are out of my mouth, I hear the door slam open and Bishop's booming voice before Kiara ends the call. I clutch my phone against my chest and try to will my heart rate to calm the hell down. I owe Kiara for this. I know her and Bish swore to never lie to each other and I have put her in the middle of my shit. I just hope Bishop doesn't take his anger out on her. I know when I do eventually go home, because there is no doubt in my mind I will go home at some point, Bishop and the others will be mad. I'm pulled from my thoughts when a knock sounds at the door. I drop my phone on the bed and head to the door to collect my room service. I yank the door open, not even bothering to check the peephole, and my blood turns to ice when I lock eyes with espresso-colored ones.

"We need to talk." The sound of his voice pulls me from my shock. I try to slam the door closed but he shoves it back sending me stumbling back a few steps and I trip, falling to my ass. He comes in uninvited and closes the door. I launch to my feet and rush for the bed to get my phone to call for help. I'm inches away from grabbing it when an arm wraps around my waist and I'm hauled back against his solid chest. I attempt to scream but he clamps his free hand over my mouth muting my screams. I thrash in his hold and fight to get free, but his hold on me doesn't budge. I freeze when another knock sounds at the door. I feel him stiffen behind me for a second before I fight harder to get to the door. He bends low so his lips brush against the shell of my ear. "The more you fight, the harder I will make this, keep quiet or I'll put a bullet between your eyes right now!"

The threat in his voice is clear, even if I did get free and managed to call my brother there is no way Bishop would get to me in time before this bastard killed me. Resigned to my fate I go limp in his arms. The knock sounds again. He moves us toward the door, my heart is going wild inside my chest. He drops his hand from my mouth, I open it to cry for help but clamp it closed when I feel the barrel of his gun at my side.

"Open the door, take your food, thank him and then close it. Do anything else and both you and the server boy will wind up in the dumpster out back." I roll my shoulders and slip my mask on, I know how to hide the terror like a pro. I nod my head and he uses his gun to push me forward a step so I can open the door. The young man darts his gaze between me and Vin before holding the tray out to me. I grip it with shaky hands and thank him, hoping like hell he gets out of here fast and doesn't wind up dead, like I will be soon enough. I step back, Vin closes the door and locks it, he points toward the small sitting area, and like the obedient puppy that I am, I do as he says.

I place the tray on the small table next to the window and drop into one of the two chairs. I should have trusted my gut. I thought I was overreacting when I met him on the plane, then he showed up today and I bit his head off. I shouldn't have allowed his look of shame to sway me. I should have sent him on his fucking way instead of telling him where I was staying! I led him right to my fucking door! He keeps his gun trained on me as he drops into the seat opposite me. I look from the gun to him and shake my head, God I was such a fool.

"Don't look so shocked, this was happening either way." I scoff and turn to look out the window, I refuse to let his face be the last thing I see before I die.

"Just do what it is you need to. Fair warning though, as soon as you pull that trigger you will be on the run for the rest of your life. My brothers won't stop hunting you, they will chase you down like the fucking dog you are." A humorless chuckle escapes him which draws my gaze back to his. I see it now. His mask is gone and his eyes shine with hatred and bloodlust.

"Your brothers are next, rest assured they will suffer for their crimes." Anger like I have never felt before surges inside me.

"You lay one fucking finger on them—" He moves so fast I have no time to prepare. He's bent over the table with the gun pressed against my forehead in a second. His breaths come in short, rapid pants, his eyes darkened to the point they almost look black. "Pull the trigger, see what hell you unleash on yourself then, you fucking creep."

"Your family is a fucking disease and so are the rest of those bottom feeding cockroaches. You are going to be the start of their demise." Fear chokes me. I can see it in his eyes that his threats aren't empty, he will kill me, I have no doubt about that. I search his gaze, trying to find a shred of humanity inside him, or even the guy who talked to me for hours on the plane. I may be dense but even I could tell he wasn't faking that, he was genuine and... nice.

"Why are you doing this? I've never done anything to you," I whisper hoping to get him talking so I can buy some time to figure out a way to get out of here.

"Take your robe off, lay on the bed." Everything inside me stills, uncontrollable fear grips me and has me seeing dark spots in my vision, I can't breathe.

Chapter Five

Vincent

I dart around the table and manage to catch her just in time before she hits the floor. She fucking passed out!

I growl as I lift her into my arms, her tiny frame is limp as I hold her bride style. I look down at her and freeze, her robe has parted and I see the purple lace of her panties and bra, her skin like silk. I just want to run my finger along the curves of her body. A small moan tumbles from her lips pulling me from my thoughts. I make my way over to the bed and position her in the middle. I look around the room and when I spot the lamps on either side of the bed, I make quick work of ripping the cords from each of them before using them to tie her hands to each of the bed posts.

I grab the chair I was just sitting on and drag it to the end of the bed, take a seat and rest my forearms on my thighs and just wait. I should take the photo's now whilst she is tied up and unconscious, that would be the perfect photos to send to her brothers. Question is, why the fuck am I not taking those photos right now?

There was something in her eyes when I told her to strip. All the color drained from her face, she was pale as a ghost. I felt how cold she was in my arms, shivers thrumming through her tiny body. Having a gun in her face didn't even scare her to that degree but the thought of dropping her robe petrified her.

"Stop, please... no more." My eyes snap to hers as she thrashes around yanking on the restraints, then comes to with a gut-wrenching scream. I jump on the bed climbing on top of her before clamping a hand over her mouth. Tears are streaming down her cheeks. Her gaze is unfocused, it takes her a minute to focus again. When her eyes finally clear and she sees me—it shocks the fuck out of me when she relaxes. I search her gaze trying to find a tell as to what the fuck is going through her mind but I can't see anything other than relief.

"If I move my hand from your mouth, are you gonna scream?" She instantly shakes her head. I keep my hand there for a minute longer before slowly removing it and sitting back on my haunches. It's now that I notice I'm straddling her. I keep my face blank and gaze on her, waiting to see what her reaction will be. The way she behaved before and how she is acting now isn't right. Something more is going on with her and I always get the facts before the final shot.

She runs her gaze over me and I see nothing but fear and loathing in her eyes. I can point a gun to her head and get nothing more than annoyance in her eyes and yet now, she looks at me like she is sizing me up for a fight. "You passed out." Fuck knows why I just stated the obvious but I felt compelled to fill the silence.

"Figures." I expected her to lash out and make threats, not resign herself to my mercy. "Just do whatever it is you need to do." The dejected tone of her voice tells me she will comply, her earlier fight is drained from her. She turns her head to the side and closes her eyes. I climb off her and reclaim my seat at the end of the bed. She doesn't clamp her legs closed or even move an inch, I've seen this shit too many fucking times to turn a blind eye. I've killed men for even thinking of touching a woman in the way I now know Carlina has been touched.

"Who did it?" She doesn't move a muscle or even bat an eyelid at my question. This girl thinks I'm about to use her body for my own pleasure and is trying to detach herself mentally to avoid the pain. Disgust rolls through me, I would never touch a woman who is unwilling. "I'll ask one more time nicely, then I'll pry the fucking answer from you." She turns her head and opens her eyes as she gazes up at the ceiling refusing to even look at me. "Who touched you?" The defiant scoff that comes from her has me clenching my hands into fists. I'm not used to being back chatted or even having a conversation with anyone aside from Marco.

"No one laid a fucking finger on me!" The hate that laces each of her words tells me she is so full of shit. I won't push her on it, instead I stand from my chair and leave to go next door to grab my laptop. I'm testing her to see if she will scream or try something, I've never taken on a job where it involves killing a woman. This is a first for me. The only reason I'm here is because of her last name and who she is related to. I grab my laptop and belongings from my room before heading back to hers. She didn't make a sound or even move an inch. I think she may be having a mental breakdown or something.

"You and I are gonna pack your shit, then we are going on a little road trip." That has her head lifting and locking eyes with me. Hers are dark and filled with malice. I hate that a part of me relishes in the fact she has some fight back in her eyes instead of a weak pathetic scared little girl.

"I'm not going anywhere with you—" Her mouth snaps shut when I pull my gun and point it at her.

"Play by my rules and I won't hurt you. Defy me or push me and you will suffer for it." Her eyes spark with fire, she is an oddity for sure. A gun in her face pushes her to rebel but the thought of me undressing her shuts her down. I will find out who hurt her and end them after I deal with this... situation.

I pack all her things and clear out the bathroom of all her feminine products. I expected her to have more shit than she does but I'm not complaining. Once everything is inside her suitcase, I look over at her and curse beneath my breath. I sort through her bag and find a pair of jeans and a vintage tee with an old rock band on it. I toss the clothes on the end of the bed before moving toward her right side. I grip the cord and look down at her. She refuses to meet my gaze so I reach out, grip her chin and force her to face me.

"You will change and act like a fucking lady as we leave. Cause a scene and I give you my word, I will put a fucking bullet in whoever you try to wrangle to help you. Nod if you understand." Her upper lip curls in anger but she nods. I untie her arms and watch as she sits up rubbing her wrists and shakes out her hands to circulate the flow of blood again. The sound of her phone ringing draws both of our attention. I narrow my eyes in warning. She slips off the bed, gathers her clothes and moves toward the bathroom. I block her path and glare down at her. "Nice try, Gucci, you change here."

"No way!" she shrieks. I cross my arms over my chest, making sure to keep my gun clutched in my grip in case she tries something. We stand here for a good few minutes glaring at each other before she does a weird high pitch squeal thing and stomps her foot like a fucking child, then turns back toward the bed. She lays the clothes on the edge of the bed before pulling the jeans on under her robe. she peers back at me over her shoulder and sighs.

Yeah, I'm not looking away to give you a chance to run—

My thought is cut off when she drops the robe to the floor and I see the cigarette burns on her lower back. I unknowingly move toward her shoving my gun in my waistband before gripping her hips. She gasps in shock, her grip on the shirt in her hands tightens but she doesn't pull away. I swipe my thumbs over the burns and anger boils inside me. I spin her around to face me. Her eyes are wide with shock, her lacy bra brushes against me, as she cranes her neck back to meet my gaze.

"Who did that to you?" She nibbles on her bottom lip for a moment before dropping her gaze and sidestepping me to pull her shirt on. I stand here and watch as she retrieves some sandals from her suitcase and zips the bag up. This girl is a fucking puzzle and I need to solve it. Once she has her shoes on, I grab my duffle and shove my laptop inside. I motion for her to grab her own bags because I'm not carrying that shit. She rolls her eyes but does as she is told. I grab her phone and shove it in my pocket before leading us from the room. Once in the hallway I motion for her to lead us toward the elevators. I'll admit, I did watch her ass the whole way.

Chapter Six

Carlina

As soon as the elevator doors open in the lobby I step out, and assume we are heading toward the exit but when he grunts behind me, I turn to find him nodding toward the back exit. I take a calming breath and do as he says. The warm air hits me as soon as I step out back. Vin grips my arm and leads me down the street until we stop beside a white Kia sport. I eye the car and then look at him, his blank stare grating on my nerves. He pulls a key from his pocket and unlocks the car before opening the trunk. If he thinks I'm getting in there he has another freaking thing coming.

He places his bag inside, then reaches for mine. I relax slightly knowing I won't be able to fit in there with the bags.

He closes the trunk, then opens the door for me to sit shot-gun. I scanned the area as we were walking, there is no one around and nowhere for me to cover if he chose to shoot at me when I ran.

Resigned to my fate I slip inside the car and buckle my seatbelt as he rounds the car and hops in. Neither of us say a word as he drives us out of the city. I have no idea where the hell we are going. A part of me is scared shitless he is taking me to the middle of nowhere to kill me and leave my body out there for the bugs to feast on. God, I could just imagine what my brothers would do if they found me dead in the outback of fuck-knows-where.

I rest my forehead against the window and allow myself to wallow. The one time I get my freedom and I don't even last a whole fucking day on my own! I have no idea who the fuck this guy is or why he is doing this.

"Is your name even Vin?" I ask. I can feel his gaze boring into the side of my head but I ignore it. I thought I was smart, thought I didn't need my brothers to protect me, but I was so fucking wrong. This guy is probably going to rape me and then kill me just to send a message to Bishop. I'm no fucking queen... I'm just a pawn in this game of power these men like to play.

"Vincent." For some unknown reason knowing that he didn't lie about his name makes me feel semi connected to him. Bish always said if you can connect with someone you can survive them. Maybe, just freaking maybe, I might be able to get the hell out of here with my life.

I'm roused awake by Vin shaking me. I rub my eyes and look around not being able to see anything thanks to it still being dark out, the only light coming from the moon. I don't know how long I was asleep but I'm still so exhausted, crashing after my adrenaline rush earlier I think. I slowly turn to face Vin, his eyes are hooded and I can see exhaustion is weighing heavy on him. I run my gaze over him trying to get a better read of who he is. He looks like a normal guy, albeit a freaking hot guy but at first glance he doesn't give off killer vibes. I saw the killer inside him when I mentioned my brothers earlier which tells me he isn't here for me, he's here because of who I share DNA with.

"Get out," he orders. Too tired to argue or put up a fight, I do as he says. He heads toward the trunk so I do the same grabbing my bags out at the same time he gets his. I follow after him and take in my surroundings. We are in the middle of what looks to be like a jungle. We walk for a bloody long time, my feet are aching and my arms are sore from carrying my suitcase and bag. It must be early hours of the morning but the humidity is killer, sweat dripping off me. I'm about ready to demand we take a break when I spot a light ahead. I furrow my brow, surprised that there is electricity out here in the middle of the jungle.

Vin stops so suddenly I crash into the back of him, nearly falling to my ass but he swings around and catches me around my waist. We stare at each other without uttering a word before he steadies me and quickly steps back.

I stand here and watch as he turns to a large tree beside us, pulls the big green leaves out of the way to reveal a small cut out in the side of its trunk. What in the ever-loving hell? He turns a switch and then puts the leaves back into positions. Unable to hold my tongue I ask.

"What was that?" He flicks his gaze over me briefly

before grabbing his bags and walking off with me hot on his heels.

"It switches off the security to the perimeter." My brows jump up in surprise, who the fuck is this guy?

As we clear the trees, I see a small... hut. Vin continues on ahead while I stand here and just stare. He climbs the two steps and pauses at the front door before turning back to me. "I guarantee that you will never find your way back to the car. Either come in or stay out here with the wildlife." I debate my options for two seconds before closing the distance between us. As soon as I reach the porch step the security light shuts off and we are plunged into darkness. I wish I could say that the dark doesn't scare me but I'm not a liar. I huddle in closer to Vin. I don't miss the way his body tenses at my proximity. He unlocks the door, steps inside and flicks some switches to his right then the room is illuminated by light.

"Holy shit." Vin spins to face me but I'm too busy dropping my bags at the door and pushing past him to take in the room. The outside has moss and vines covering it from what I could see. I expected the inside to be like a hunting cabin but it's so far from that. The inside is open and bright, with a small kitchen, a couch and TV, a queen bed and... a bath? I spin around and that's when I notice there are no doors inside, it may be beautiful and airy with new furniture decorated in cream and brown tones but a girl needs her privacy!

"Something on your mind, Gucci?" I keep my back to him. I may want to lash out and give him a piece of my mind but I'm also not dumb. He has a gun and is twice the size of me. He could crush me with his bare hands if he wanted to. I'm torn from my inner debate when I feel him pressed against my back. "Say whatever is on your mind." His whispered words has a shiver rolling down my treacherous body, goose flesh dotting my arms and the hair on the back of my neck raising.

"W-why are there no doors?" I croak, his nearness throwing me off.

"I eliminated the possibility of you being able to plan shit behind closed doors." I nod like an idiot, acting like I understand what he is saying.

"I'm not sleeping in the same bed with you," I blurt out. A deep chuckle comes from him but it's not a humorous sound it's more like a mocking laugh.

"Yeah, you are," is all he says before stepping around me and heading toward the bed to drop his bags down before turning to face me. "There is a bath there or a shower outside. There is no hot water outside." His eyes are alight with mirth which just has me grinding my teeth in annoyance.

"And?" He runs his gaze over me, not in a sexual way but as if he is appraising me.

"You stink, you're washing before you get into my bed."

"Your bed?" I balk.

"That's what I said." I can tell from the clipped tone of his voice he is getting annoyed with all my questions.

"I'll shower outside," I rush to say, making a smile spread across his handsome face.

"There is no curtain or light out there. It's around the side of the house next to the shed." He turns to head toward the bath but stops and peers over his shoulder at me. "You try to run and I promise you I will catch you before you can even make it a mile away from here." I fight the urge to gulp and just nod my head instead.

I can see it in his eyes and hear it in his tone, he means what he says and I don't doubt he will be true to his word. I just need to bide my time until I can figure out a way to get out of here and away from Vin. A towel smacking me in the face pulls me from my thoughts. I catch it before it drops to the ground and shoot him a glare. The cocky bastard ignores me and heads for the kitchen. I situate my suitcase at the end of the bed and rummage through it until I find a pair of sleep shorts and a loose tank top.

I ignore Vin as I walk out of the hut and slam the door behind me just so he knows I'm pissed. The only light is from the moon. I expect the security light to turn on when I hit the dirt but it doesn't. I follow his directions and head around the side where I can see a small shed. I come to a halt and growl when I see the metal shower head sticking out of the side of the house. I don't know what it is about the shower or if it has anything to do with it but the tears I have been battling finally fall. I let them run unchecked down my cheeks and take a moment to allow myself to feel. For the first time in my life, I wanted to be able to introduce myself using my real name and be seen, heard or even admired.

I wipe the tears from my cheeks, take a deep breath and square my shoulders. Crying will get me nowhere, but planning an escape and fighting for my freedom will be worth dying for. I refuse to be a helpless scared little girl. I'll prove to myself that I can survive this overbearing asshole and be the fucking queen I know I can be.

Chapter Seven

Vincent

From the moment she walked out the door I have been watching her on the cameras that surround this place. She may think because of where we are that we are cut off. I'll allow her to think that, what she doesn't know is we have full cell service and WIFI. We actually do have a detachable shower head in the bath, but I wasn't going to tell her that. I watch as she leans against the house with her towel and clothes clutched to her chest crying. A pang of guilt hits me but I quickly push that away. I should have strapped her to a chair and tortured the information from her but I just can't bring myself to fucking do it... and there lies the fucking problem!

My phone rings and I pull my gaze from my laptop and check the caller ID before answering.

"What have you got for me Marco?"

"Nothing much. All I have been able to find out is Carlina Murdoch never existed until a few months after her father's death. She was spotted in public with her brothers, went to school but under a different name. She has been kept hidden for years and I don't know why that would be." I grip my phone tighter in anger, I know exactly why she was hidden from the world.

"Tony was keeping her a secret, the cunt had an ace up his sleeve the whole fucking time."

"I'm not following here, brother."

"Tony was going to use her when the time was right to marry her off to one of the families to ensure an alliance." I look back to the screen and lift my hand to slam it closed when she begins to undress but I don't. She has no idea I'm watching her and yet she has my full attention. She drops her jeans and shirt to the ground. She remains in her panties and bra as she flicks the shower on and––.

"Vincent?" I clear my throat and quickly, then shut the lid before focusing back on Marco.

"Yeah?"

"What do you plan to do with her?"

"Exactly what I was hired to do, finish the fucking job." The sound of my cousin scoffing on the other end of the line has anger brewing inside me.

"If that were true, she would have been dead hours ago." I close my eyes and take a calming breath. Marco knows me better than anyone in this world. "Why is she still breathing, Vincent?" The firmness of his tone tells me he is worried I'm digging myself a hole I won't be able to climb out of.

"She isn't what the job sheet said and there—"

"It doesn't fucking matter!" he whisper shouts. "She is a Murdoch and you being near her, fuck, you kidnapping her is putting a fucking target on your back. You went dark years ago, everyone thinks you are fucking dead, Vin. Are you willing to come back from the dead for a piece of washed-up pussy that will never be yours?" His words ring true, I have asked myself more times than I can count since meeting Carlina. What the fuck am I doing? This girl isn't like she has been portrayed to be, something about her calls to a part of me I thought had died a long time ago when my sister went missing. "Carlina Murdoch isn't Selena, Vin." His whispered words hit me right in the chest. All the air rushes from my lungs at the mention of my sister's name, a name I haven't heard or spoken aloud in over ten years.

"I know she isn't," I reply barely above a whisper. I try to push away the sadness and guilt whenever the thought of my sister arises.

"Then end this, brother. Do what you do best and put a bullet in her head and disappear, Vincent." I hear his words and know what he is saying is true, then why the fuck can't I bring myself to do it? What the fuck is it about this girl that has me pausing and slowing down to think. I don't think, that's what makes me one of the best mercenaries in the world. I'm cold, calculated. I feel nothing and don't fear death. I hear the sound of her soft foot fall on the steps outside. I rush to tell Marco I'll check in when it's done before ending the call.

The door opens and I fight to keep my face blank, her long brown hair is wet and dripping down her front, I drop my gaze and fight a groan, her nipples are hard and poking through her shirt. Her stomach is on display, her shorts are so fucking tiny they barely cover her pussy! She moves toward the bed and I sit here watching her every move. I can see her trying to look inconspicuous about taking in her surroundings but I notice.

She drops her clothes on the foot of the bed and I bite down on my tongue, her purple bra and panties sit there displayed proudly on top of her clothes. She stalks toward the chairs at the table and drapes her wet towel over the back. My greedy eyes zero in on the fact I can see the bottom of her ass cheeks hanging out of her shorts. She has her shorts high enough that the waistband covers the burns marks that mark her beautiful body.

When she turns around her eyes zone in on the end of the bed. I follow her gaze and smirk. She's just noticed she left her panties and bra out in the open for me to see. A blush works its way up her neck and hits her cheeks as she rushes over and quickly gathers them in her arms before stuffing them inside her suitcase. I fight the laughter that wants to bubble out of me and stand, reach around to grip the back of my shirt and pull it off.

I cut a glance to her and find her eyes glued to my naked torso. This girl is like no other. She should be screaming and crying, begging for her life. She does none of that and stands there openly checking me out. I don't bother to even speak as I grab a towel and some clothes, then head outside for a shower, the cold water will do me a world of good.

***

I pull on a pair of gray shorts and gather my discarded clothes before making my way back inside. I had no worry of her escaping. The motion sensors around the property would have sounded the alarm if she did try to run. I climb the steps and push open the door, expecting to find her chewing her nails or looking for a knife to kill me with. What I didn't expect was the sight in front of me. She has pulled the blanket and a pillow from the bed and set herself up on the two-seater couch where she is currently asleep. I grind my teeth as I make my way over to where the bath is and push against the wooden wall, it's a hidden door where the laundry room is and the toilet. She has no idea it's there and I can't wait to see her face when she thinks she has to take a shit in the woods.

I close the door behind me and move to the other side of the bed where another hidden door is, I lay my hand flat against it and push. This wall slides out to reveal my three monitors and all my files I have on my kills and future jobs I may be interested in. I grab the file I have from Carlina and slot it in with the rest, I don't trust her not to snoop through my things. I close the compartment and stand here staring at her. Her brows are drawn in and I can tell she isn't having a good sleep. Just as I decide to leave her where she is and get some sleep myself, she groans, and begins to mutter under her breath. I move closer to her, wanting to hear what she is saying.

"No, stop it! Tony don't." Hearing her father's name slip from her lips has rage coursing through me. She looks so innocent and untouchable laying in front of me. The grimace on her face alerts me to the fact she is dreaming about some of the horrors she must have faced at the hands of her father.

When her tiny hands clench the comforter, I'm done for. I slide my hands beneath her body and lift her into my arms with the blanket still draped over top of her. A small whimper spills from her full lips. The five steps it takes from the couch to the bed she relaxes in my arms. I place her gently on the bed before grabbing the pillow off the couch, flicking the lights off, then slipping in beside her. I make sure to keep enough space between us. I roll onto my back and rest my arm behind my head as I stare up at the ceiling trying to sort through my thoughts. I have never hesitated on a kill before.

Tonight, she was supposed to disrobe and lay on the bed so I could snap some photos and use them to bait her brother. But, the look in her eyes and the fact she passed out change everything. She is my ticket to finding my sister. Selena is the only reason I still stick around and don't move across the fucking world to New Zealand. There is still a chance I could rescue my sister. I know the chance is slim to fucking none but I need to figure out where the fuck Tony sent her. Once the Murdoch's are dealt with, I'm going after my father. He will die painfully for ever thinking he had the fucking right to sell my sister for his own fucking gain!

Chapter Eight

Carlina

I kick the blankets off trying to escape the heat and cool down. My body is burning up but I can't seem to cool down. When I try to move, I freeze. My eyes snap open and I'm met with the sight of a naked chest! Looking down, I find my hand resting flat against a set of abs, his arm draped over me and my leg sandwiched in between his large ones. I tilt my head back to look up at him and I squeal. His eyes are open and on me. I shove away from him and scramble to the other side of the bed, mortified I was fucking snuggled up next to my captor!

"Didn't pick you for the cuddly type." I can't even look at him, feeling sick knowing that I slept next to him. I bite my lip to keep my tears at bay. I need to get the hell out of here. As if fate heard my very thoughts my phone begins to ring. I dart my gaze to the kitchen counter then back to Vin. His eyes narrow in warning, fuck it.

I launch off the bed and race toward the kitchen. I hear him behind me but don't stop, if this is my only chance at escaping him, I need to take it. I grip my phone and answer Kiara's call. I'm about to scream for help but clamp my mouth closed when I feel the barrel of his gun pressed to the back of my head. He leans forward to whisper in my ear low enough Kiara won't be able to hear.

"Say everything is fine and make it believable." His breath fanning across my exposed skin sends an involuntary shiver down my spine. With how close he is to me, I know he felt it. "Put it on speaker." With shaky fingers I do as he says.

"Car!" I cringe at the loud shout.

"I-I'm here," I say, and hear Kiara sigh in relief.

"I have like five minutes before he finds me." I cringe, hating that she is going behind my brother's back to help me. I'm such a bitch.

"What's going on?"

"Bishop got Luka to track you." My shoulders droop but then it occurs to me, if Bish knows where I am then he will also know Vin has kidnapped me. I make sure to keep the excitement off my face and out of my voice. "Luka hacked the hotel feed. Bish is pissed."

"Why?"

"Uh, your brother saw you leaving the hotel last night with your bags and... a guy." This is good, at least Bishop knows what Vince looks like and he will be able to find me now. "Problem is, the guy's back is to the camera the whole time. Bishop wanted a face ID so he could run a background check." The hope flees my body, Vin knew exactly what he was doing that's why he took the back exit. "Car?"

"Yeah?" I can hear the disappointment in my own voice and hope to hell Kiara doesn't pick up on it.

"I'll handle Bishop, just make sure you send a picture every second day so I know you're okay." I nod even though she can't see me. "Also, send a pic of the guy you've taken off with." She laughs and I try to do the same but my laughter is forced and hollow. "Shit, he's coming, speak soon." She ends the call and the tears I fought to hide fall freely. Vince rips my phone from my hand and I don't even protest. I silently walk toward the door, throw it open, then drop down onto the top step as I bury my face in my hands and cry. A sharp cry tears from me when I'm pulled to my feet by my hair. Vin wraps his hand around my throat and shoves me hard against the wall of the house, then bends and gets right in my face.

"You fucking pull a stunt like that again and you'll regret it." I claw at his forearm fighting him. I can't breathe, and the anger in his eyes tells me he has reached his breaking point. Right as spots begin to dance in my vision, he drops his hold. I crumble to the floor like a sack of shit gasping for air and rubbing at my throat. Tears cascade down my cheeks as I drag in lungful after lungful of air. He grips my hair again and wrenches my head back so I'm staring up at him. "Don't fucking push me, Carlina. You won't like what I will do to you." My bottom lip trembles. He releases me with a hard shove and storms back inside the house, slamming the door closed behind him.

I've sat outside all day refusing the food he has offered and the water he brought out. I want to claw his fucking eyes out and stab his face for laying his hands on me. I wrap my arms around my legs and rest my chin on top as I watch the sunset. I've done nothing but sit here and try to come up with a plan of escape. All I have to do is wait for him to fall asleep, then make a break for it through the jungle.

I can't remember how many turns we took on foot to get here but it can't be that hard to find my way back to the car, then to the main road to flag someone down for help. I can't just sit here and wait to die. I need to do something or at the very least try. With my mind made up I shakily climb to my feet and head inside. I spot him out of the corner of my eye sitting at the table on his laptop. Ignoring him I ruffle through my case to find a pair of yoga pants, socks and a T-shirt. I snag my toothbrush and paste as well. I make sure to place my runners strategically on top before closing the lid and not zipping it. I need to make the least amount of noise possible tonight and have everything ready to go. I grab my towel from the back of the other chair, and without sparing him a glance, walk outside to the shower. It's hot enough out here that I don't care about not having hot water.

I strip off quickly, then tie my hair up so it doesn't get wet. Turning the shower on, I quickly step under the spray and use the pump soap I left out here last night to wash my body. I brush my teeth before turning the shower off, then dry myself and change into the clothes I brought with me. I decide to leave the socks off and plan to put them on when I fake going to bed. Nerves are rattling me. I got a taste of what he is capable of today, so I won't lie and say I'm not scared shitless because I am.

I climb the steps and take a deep breath, giving myself a mental pep talk to get my game face on and act like none of this bothers me. As long as I remain calm and don't let him see through my mask everything should be fine... I hope. I open the door and immediately spot him in the kitchen, the aromas wafting toward me have my stomach grumbling and his gaze snapping toward me. I quickly turn away from him and march over to my suitcase with my head held high, it's going to suck leaving my stuff behind but materialistic things can be replaced, my life can't be.

"Dinner will be ready in five minutes. You will be eating." I keep my back to him and nod. If I have to suffer through dinner with the asshole then so be it. Whatever he is making smells good and I know I will need the energy for the long night ahead. I stuff my clothes in my case and place my socks discreetly inside my shoes before closing the lid, still leaving it unzipped. I play my part well and take a seat at the table he has already set with cutlery and glasses of water. I peek over at him and hate the fact I still find him handsome. He may be a bastard who hurt me but I can't lie and say he isn't easy on the eye. What is it with me and asshole men. The only good men I know in my life are my brothers. Each of them loves me with all they have and I them. I shake myself out of my thoughts when Vin makes his way toward me with two plates in his hands. He places one in front of me and takes his seat with the other.

There are a range of different vegetables that are bright and vibrant in color. The meat is cooked well done with a buttery sauce that coats it. This meal looks fit for a restaurant, the presentation beautiful. I'll admit I'm slightly surprised that this brute can actually cook a decent meal. I'd pictured someone like him out back with a deer strung up, skinning it, then eating it raw. I eye my plate not willing to eat it in case he has poisoned it or something. He sighs then reaches over to switch our plates.

"Happy now?" I narrow my eyes as I grip my knife and fork staring at him.

"Ecstatic," I quip as I cut into my steak. The meat melts in my mouth, the taste has an appreciative moan tearing out of me before I can stop it. I snap my gaze to his, mortified. His eyes are on me, his mouth open with his fork paused midair. I gulp down the meat and drop my gaze back to my plate dying of embarrassment. I shovel the food into my mouth for something to do other then sit here in awkward silence with my captor. He clears his throat trying to garner my attention but I refuse to lift my gaze, I've already made a fool of myself and don't need to tempt fate.

"This morning—" I cut him off before he can continue, not wanting to hear the bullshit he is about to spill.

"Let's move on, water under the bridge and all that." I stand grabbing my plate to dump in the sink. As I'm about to pass him, he reaches out and grips my forearm. His grip isn't tight, it's just... there. I keep my face blank as I slowly turn to face him, just like me he is shielding his thoughts behind a mask. Neither of us wants the other to know what our next move is. The thing is, the ball is in his freaking court since he is the bloody one who took me!

"Whatever you are thinking of trying..." His eyes narrow in warning as I fight to keep my expression blank, when the whole time my heart is beating so fast. I'm surprised he can't hear it. "I highly recommend you don't do anything stupid." I nod my head swiftly. He drops his grip on me and I dash into the kitchen away from him to try to calm my racing heart. I don't know how he knows or if he is just guessing, but I know now without a doubt I have to do this, tonight.

Chapter Nine

Vincent

I feign sleep, waiting for her to make her move. She thinks she is slick and able to pull one over on me.

Stupid girl.

I knew something was up from the moment she walked back inside today. I could see the cogs in her mind working overtime. If that didn't give it away the fact that she left her runners on top of her clothes and didn't zip her case did the trick. I thought she would come to her senses after her shower, but when she walked back in and tried to be discreet about stuffing her socks in her running shoes...! That told me she was going to make her move.

The thrill of chasing her down excites the fuck out of

me. It shouldn't, but knowing I will get to make her submit to me calls to a dark part inside my dead soul. We went to bed at least three hours ago, her inner thoughts are so fucking loud I can hear them. She would make a shit spy. She is stiff and has been laying on the edge of the bed the whole time. If she thought she was doing good at acting like she was sleeping, she is wrong. The girl hogged the fucking bed and blankets last night. She fights like a fucking ninja in her sleep. I keep still and make sure my breathing remains the same as she slowly inches out of the bed. I plan to let her run for a while before I drag her ass back, nothing worse than thinking you got away only for it to be yanked from your grasp.

The floor creaks once her feet hit the ground. She stills and I can feel her gaze on me watching, waiting to see if I react. Tense minutes tick by before she finally moves again. I hear the lid of her suitcase lift then slowly close again a second later. I hear her pad softly toward the door, then hear the lock turn and the door slowly opening. I strain my hearing after the door closes, hearing her creep down the steps and then the sound of footfalls hitting the dirt has me jumping from the bed, grabbing my discarded shirt from the floor and grabbing my own shoes and gun before going after her.

I break through the first line of trees and stop, squint my eyes and follow the tracks she's left behind. My blood is pumping and excitement rolls through me as the hunter in me takes over. I take off, following her tracks in the wet ground. She is a city girl and has no idea that the footprints she leaves behind in the moist ground are like a neon sign with her location. Her tracks lead east toward the river where I fish. I run eating up the space between us and within mere minutes I'm right on her tail. I come to a halt behind a kapok tree and watch her. The moonlight illuminates her figure as she stands there looking left to right, trying to gain her bearings. She hasn't even made it ten minutes from the house and is already lost. She gets some respect for at least trying to run but she is a fool. She should have tried to scout the area on the way in and left a trail of some sort to follow back to the car.

She turns and heads right causing me to shake my head, she should have gone left and that would have lead her in the direction of the car. I follow after her, keeping my foot steps in time with her small ones so she doesn't hear me following her. I watch her from afar and admire the fact that even though she has no fucking idea where she is going or what she is doing, she doesn't give up. She stops, again, and I shake my head. If I were anyone else she would be fucking dead. She hasn't taken stock of her surroundings or even checked to make sure she isn't being followed. Her family did her a fucking disservice by not training her for an encounter like this. She should have been able to disarm me and put me on my ass in her hotel room.

"Shit," she curses, this fucking girl! Tired of watching her flounder her way through the jungle, I close in. She is hunched over trying to catch her breath. She doesn't hear or see me coming. When she straightens, I strike. I press against her back and reach around her front to grip her tiny neck in my grasp and squeeze. She screams and I allow it. She tries to fight me but it's futile. I wrap my other arm around her midriff and mold her to my front. "Let me go!"

"Scream all you want, Gucci, no one will hear your cries. We are miles away from anyone. I could fuck you right here and no one would come help you." She freezes, her screams mute and it's then I recall my words and mentally berate myself for letting that slip. I would be a liar if I said she wasn't beautiful and the thought of fucking hasn't crossed my mind... because it has, a lot.

"Don't." Her broken plea strikes a chord within me. I bend so my lips brush against the shell of her ear, she may be terrified of me but her body betrays her as a shiver runs down her spine.

"Why did you try to run?" I whisper huskily.

"Why wouldn't I? You've taken me against my will, held me at gunpoint and told me to strip for you. What other choice did I have?" Her words are steady and sure but the slight tremble in her hands gives her away. I spin her around and drive her back three steps until her back is against a palm tree. I grip her throat and get right in her face. The defiant look in her eyes spurs me on. I push her higher against the tree so her legs dangle in the air. I wait for her to panic and beg, claw at my arm or something but she shocks the fuck out of me when she reaches out, grips my shoulders—using them as leverage—to hoist herself up enough to lock her legs around my waist. My grip on her drops as I wrap my arms around her to keep her from falling. Why the fuck my instinct is to protect her from falling, I have no fucking idea.

"What the fuck are you doing?" I snarl up at her. The dirty little minx looks as shocked as I am at her bold move. She quickly wipes the look from her face and stares at me with a sinful look in her eyes that has my grip on her tightening and my cock growing hard.

"Turning the tables." I furrow my brow confused at what the hell she is saying. To make matters worse, I'm losing my focus and picturing fucking her against the tree where I had her pinned moments ago. She runs her hands along my shoulders before reaching around the back of my neck, gripping a fist full of my hair and tugs. An unwarranted groan spills from my lips. Her eyes widen an inch, I need to snap the fuck out of it. I release my hold on her expecting her to land on her ass in front of me but she doesn't. She tightens her hold around my waist and grips my hair tighter.

"Get the fuck off me now!" I grit out through clenched teeth.

"See, I would believe you but..." Her cunning eyes spark with fire and I grind my teeth to keep myself from snapping her fucking pretty little neck. She leans down so her full lips ghost over mine. I stand completely still unsure of what the fuck I am supposed to do. "I can feel how hard you are for... me." Her sultry words pull me from my stupor. I slam against the tree and relish in the hiss that escapes her when I grind my hardness against her core. A moan tumbles from her lips, and without thought my body reacts and I slam my lips against hers. She gasps, giving me entry and allowing me to swipe my tongue across hers. The taste of her hits my senses and I moan at the taste. She pushes against my chest. I pull back but the dirty little devil clamps her teeth down on my bottom lip drawing blood. I yank backward slipping free of her hold and hiss. She staggers on her feet, pinning me with a glare.

"You fucking bit me!" I snap while glaring at her. She places her hands on her hips and pins me with a look that a mother would her intolerant child.

"You kissed me!" she shouts like I wasn't fucking present during the kiss.

Chapter Ten

Carlina

"You were fucking begging for it!" My mouth drops open in horror, this freaking asshole is so full of himself! How dare he bloody kiss me without my consent. "You more pissed I kissed you or that you actually liked it?" My jaw hits the jungle floor. He uses his thumb to swipe the blood from his lip and smirks at me. I clamp my mouth closed and cross my arms over my chest in anger, then stomp my foot in frustration.

"You are so... so dumb." His brows jump high enough to hit his hairline. I expect him to rant and berate me but what I don't expect is for him to throw his head back and laugh.

My eyes zone in on his neck and imagine myself licking a trail along it until I reach his soft lips—cut that shit out! I scold myself shocked my thoughts wondered *there*. I stand here scowling at Vincent until his laughter finally dies off. He looks at me and shakes his head.

"You have two options. Follow me back willingly or I drag you back unconscious. Which will it be?" I look at him skeptically, something is off. He should be punishing me or beating the shit out of me for running.

"Why aren't you... doing something?" He cocks his head to the side running his gaze lazily over my body before finally settling on eyes before he answers.

"Gucci, I knew you were going to run from the moment I brought you here. Frankly, I'm surprised you didn't try last night." I eye him for a moment, trying to figure out what game he is playing. I can't get a read on him and that unnerves me.

"So, you're not going to... kill me?" His relaxed expression morphs instantly. I see the killer in his eyes causing me to back up a step until my back is flat against the tree. Vin crowds me, caging me in by placing his hands on either side of my head. He leans down so our noses are nearly touching, his eyes burning with intensity.

"You get one free pass. You try to run again and next time I'll take the shot, Gucci." He pushes off the tree and stalks back the way I came. I last two seconds before chasing after him. His knowing chuckle grates on my nerves. He may think he won this round but he has another thing coming if he thinks I won't try to run again. Next time, I'll be more prepared.

We haven't spoken a word to each other since last night. Sleeping next to him after kissing him back was freaking awkward. This morning neither of us said a word as we got ready for the day. He's currently in the kitchen fixing lunch whilst I avoid him outside on the porch. He was kind enough to show me where the toilet was this morning and I'll be honest, I nearly cried tears of joy knowing I didn't have to pee in the bush. I don't know what the hell came over me last night or what I had hoped to achieve, but it sure as hell wasn't him kissing me or feeling his hard cock grinding against my pussy. My body responded to him like I was a puppet obeying its master.

"You eating out here?" I peer over my shoulder to look at him and nearly swallow my fucking tongue. He stands there in a pair of dark jeans with no freaking shirt! The man has a body that will have women all over the world falling to their knees just to worship him. My mouth salivates at the sight of his indented V... my God the way... He clears his throat pulling me from my thoughts and causing me to snap my gaze back to his. The knowing look in his eyes causes a blush to coat my cheeks. I just got freaking caught checking him out!

"I-I." I clear my throat and climb to my feet as I brush off my shorts to give me something to do other than look at him. "I'll eat inside." I peek up at him through my lashes and roll my eyes when I see a ghost of a smirk on his face. I move past him, making sure to shoulder check him on my way inside. Since last night, the angry tension between us has eased and been replaced by... sexual tension that shouldn't be there!

I head over to the table and drop down into my seat with the grace of an infant elephant. I ignore Vin as he plates our food before walking toward me. He places a plate in front of me before claiming his seat. The food smells divine. It's something so simple yet it has my mouth watering for a whole different reason. I look over at him and smile wide.

"You made grilled cheese?" A smug smirk graces his handsome face, his eyes twinkle with something I can't decipher.

"I was in the mood for a... *snack.*" I gasp stunned by his boldness. I'm not stupid enough to pretend there wasn't a sexual innuendo in his meaning. I feel a blush working its way up my neck and quickly duck my head, using my hair as a curtain to shield my face from his view. I freeze when he reaches over and tucks my hair behind my ear. I slowly raise my eyes to his, taken back by the gentleness in the way he just touched me, a stark contrast to how he handled me yesterday.

"Why am I here, Vincent?" I ask softly as he drops his hand back to his lap. He stares at his plate for so long, my shoulders droop in defeat. I pick up my sandwich and nibble on it, not really tasting anything.

"Because I was hired to kill you." I choke on the bit of toast and slap my chest to help me digest it. I expected to hear him say he would kill me but not that he was hired or to hear remorse in his tone. "The people that hired me want me to strip you bare, take photos and send them to your brother to instigate a war." My stomach churns and threatens to spill the tiny amount I have eaten.

"Do you know my brother?" His eyes harden, his body turns ridged. I know the answer before he even voices it.

"Your family took something from me and I want it back." The conviction in his voice tells me he won't stop until he gets whatever *it* is back.

"Were you really hired or are you just here to piss

Bishop off and kill me in the process?" I'm beyond proud at the fact my voice doesn't quiver and I found the strength within myself to be asking him for the truth. If I am going to make it out of here in one piece, I need to know all of the facts. He leans back and crosses his arms over his chest, whilst maintaining eye contact with me.

"I don't lie. I may dodge a question or not answer at all but I am no fucking liar." I nod, encouraging him to continue. "I work for an agency. Your name came across my... desk and I took the job without thought."

"Why?"

"Because, for you to have the last name Murdoch I knew you had to be someone important or related to them. I had no idea you were their sister. I suspected you were—" I cut him off knowing what he is about to say.

"Girlfriend, side piece, cousin, hidden baby momma?" He scrunches his face in disgust. Yeah, buddy, the feeling is mutual.

"Yeah, something like that."

"If I am a job to you, what am I worth?" His brows pull in and he tilts his head to the side confused by my question, so I explain further. "What are you getting paid to take out the secret sister no one knows exists?" Anger swims in his dark gaze.

"Why the hell do you want to know that?" I throw my hands up in the air in frustration.

"Because all I have been my whole fucking life is a ticket, or a bargaining chip if you will. My life was never my own. I was hidden, not allowed friends, had to play girlfriend to my own brothers if we were spotted together. I think I at least deserve to know how much I am fucking worth since I don't exist to the world. Could you—"

"Ten million." I snap my mouth closed and stare at him in shock. *Ten million!* "You are worth ten million euros, Carlina. Someone out there really wants to send a message to your brother."

"Who hired you, Vincent?"

Chapter Eleven

Vincent

Who hired you, Vincent?

I replay her question over and over in my mind before I decide to answer. She may think she has a right to know but truth is, she doesn't. That is the first rule of the job, you don't know who hired you. The identity of the person is always confidential no matter what. There is no excuses, no fuck ups, no nothing. Bishop is the Don. He has a lot of enemies so it would be like picking a needle from a haystack trying to narrow down who ordered the hit.

"I don't know," I answer honestly.

"Why are you being so forthcoming?" The skepticism in her voice is warranted.

"You have a right to know these things." She nods solemnly.

"Right, because I won't be around long enough to tell anyone." I roll my lips over my teeth to stop myself from smiling.

"I should have killed you before you even got on the plane to come here." Her face scrunches in confusion.

"But... why didn't you?" That is a question I'm not prepared to answer right now so I deflect.

"Starting tomorrow, I'm going to train you to fight and learn how to hack so next time you won't be easy prey."

"You're going to let me go?" I give her a don't be stupid look and watch as her shoulders slump.

"I don't know what I'm going to do. Until I have all the facts and every ounce of information I need, you will be safe, for now."

———

Carlina and I spent the rest of the afternoon with her exploring around my house. I had the motion sensors switched on just in case she tried to make a run for it again. Fool me once and all that shit. I spent my time inside, combing through the dark web to try and dig up any more information I could about her. I spoke with Marco earlier to see if he had any luck. He's still digging but he doesn't sound optimistic about our chances. He's pissed as hell at me because I won't just kill her and be done with it, his need for her end is unsettling. Marco claims to know nothing about Carlina and yet he is hell bent on me taking her out and instigating a war with her family to go after my father, Vincent Murelo Senior.

I have never doubted Marco before, not for a fucking

second. Yet, I lay here next to the sister of my enemy wondering if my own blood has set me up. I shake away those thoughts, I'm spending too much time fucking thinking about this girl! I climb out of bed, careful not to disturb her, and make my way over to the wall near her. I place my hand against the wall and once the computers are up, I get to work. I search everything there is to know about Carlina and her brothers. I even go as far back as to digging into what her father was up to and who her mother was.

I'm scouring through all the information when the sun begins to peak across the horizon. I sigh and scrub a hand down my face in frustration. So far I can't find shit on Carlina. Her brother King is Bishop's underboss and does all the dirty work for him. Bishop may be a ruthless son of a bitch but he does it for the greater good. His future father-in-law has the means and power to wipe out all of Bishop's enemies but he hasn't called upon him to do that. That tells me that the Don of the Murdoch family wants to win on his own and prove himself worthy to lead his family. He gets a small amount of my respect for that. Her twin brothers go to the school she used to with her friend Kiara. I managed to find out she has another half-brother, Gage.

"You could have just asked." I swivel around on my seat to see her sitting up in bed and staring at my monitors that have hers and her family's pictures plastered all over them. I don't bother to hide them or try to make excuses. She already knows that she is a job and it's best that she and *I* don't forget that fact.

"Would you have been honest?" I challenge. She shrugs her shoulders and yawns.

"Wouldn't know. You never gave me the chance, so I guess we'll never know." It's too fucking early in the morning for this shit. I stand and stretch out my tired, achy muscles. I cut a glance to her and find her eyes are glued to my naked torso. A smirk finds its way to my lips before I turn and head to the kitchen to switch the coffee pot on. Tired of being hot and trying to make her suffer, I decide to turn the air on. I grab the remote from the drawer in the kitchen and hit the button. "Are you freaking serious?" I quirk a brow at her in questions. "I have been sweating in places no women should ever sweat, and this whole time you have had this hut fitted with AC?"

"You behave, you get privileges. You fuck up and I take them away." Her mouth drops open and before I know it, I'm blurting words out I should never have. "Unless you want my cock in that open mouth, I'd close it." I expected her to blush, or balk at my crass words. What I didn't expect was her sassy as fuck reply.

"Baby, the needle dick God cursed you to walk this earth with wouldn't even make me gasp when you slid in." I choke on my own fucking spit!

I shoot her a glare before I go about making some damn fucking coffee. This girl is becoming a fucking pain in the ass and a distraction I don't fucking need. I don't bother to make her a cup. I pour my own and head back to my desk ignoring the scowl she shoots me. It may be petty but she needs to learn to do shit on her own. I won't wipe her ass like her family did... or maids or whoever the fuck raised her. I feel her at my back peering over my shoulder as I scan through the information I have. I need to find a link that connects Bishop to the sale of my sister. A thought hits me, I can make a trade. His sister for mine?

"You know that shit is a lie, right?" I turn and peer over my shoulder at her. She points to my screen where it says King was found sleeping out the front of cemetery a couple nights ago.

"How do you know?" She shrugs her shoulder.

"King never visits the dead. He's never even been to our mother's grave and he doesn't know anyone who would be buried there." I decide to focus on that bit of information and work an angle on King, he may just be my way in. I tap into the cemetery video surveillance and follow King's movements. The guy doesn't look like his normal brooding self, he looks distraught. He stops near a gravestone and the gasp that comes from behind me has me spinning around to focus on her. She leans across me and gets as close as she can to the monitor. Her scent assaults me, she smells like fucking cotton candy and raspberries. "Oh, King."

"What does that mean?" She points to the gravestone completely unaware of how fucking close we are now. Fuck it, if I'm not going to kill her today, I may as well enjoy the fucking time I have with her until I decide otherwise. I grip her waist and pull her to me so she is sitting on my lap. She is stiff as a board but doesn't pull out of my hold. I reach around and pause the video, I rest my chin on top of her shoulder and relish in the shiver that rolls through her delectable body. "Gucci?" She shakes her head slightly and clears her throat before answering.

"That's Christine. She's King's nutcase ex-girlfriend. The bitch was nothing more than a gold digger, but I guess he loved her in his own weird... King way." Interesting. By the looks of things King had no idea she was dead either so something more is at play here. I may not be able to get an insight into Bishop or find out anything on Carlina, but I sure as shit can work an angle on her other four brothers to find a way to get what I want.

We sit here for hours scrolling through video after video of her brothers. I bring up information I have gathered about them and she tells me if it's true or not. She even goes as far as to tell me about things that don't exactly impact her family but give me a better insight into who they are. The picture she paints of them all is hero like. I can tell from the bitterness that coats her tone when she speaks of her father that she hates him. She says they didn't really know their mom, she died when the twins were one and that's it. She was barely two when she died so she says you can't mourn someone you didn't know. Thing is, I did know Selena so I mourn the loss of my sister every fucking day.

"Wait, stop." I pause the video and try to see what she is looking at. We're no longer watching her brothers but watching Pauly, Vinny, Mike and Donny. She leans forward slightly, shimming her ass to get a closer look, I wrap my arm around her waist to keep her still but she doesn't heed my fucking warning. "Vin, I need to see—"

"You keep wiggling your ass like that and my cock is going to be rock fucking hard." She freezes and I sigh in relief, the last thing I need...My thought is cut off when the dirty minx shakes her ass again and shoots me a wink over her shoulder.

Chapter Twelve

Carlina

Three weeks later...

Vincent and I have been dancing around the tension that pulses between us for weeks. We rise at the ass crack of dawn before it's too hot and he teaches me to fight, track, defend myself, and how to build traps and bombs. After training we each shower and have breakfast before gathering as much intel on all the families, including mine. I only give him information to keep him from finding the whole truth. I don't know what his obsession is with my family but no matter what, I won't let him hurt them.

There may be raw need and sexual tension between us but neither of us trust the other enough to let our guard down. I won't lie and say the sight of him shirtless and sweating each morning as he trains me doesn't get to me. Especially when he pins me to the ground and makes me submit to him, that shit gets me wet. I am washing laundry daily, because of this bronze God, my panties never seem to stay fucking dry when he is around.

Oh my God, do I have Stockholm syndrome?

"Why would you have that?" My eyes widen as I peer over my shoulder to look at him. Whenever we work together my seat is always on his lap. I'm never allowed my own chair. I mean, I'm not exactly opposed to feeling the hard ridges of his muscles pressed up against me or feeling his thick thighs beneath. Shit! I'm fucking wet again.

"I need to stop saying shit out loud," I grumble which just causes him to laugh and me to huff out my annoyance. His grip around my waist tightens as he pulls me back flush against his chest burying his nose in my hair. He seems to do that a lot, almost like he can't get enough of my smell or touching me. He has been finding any chance he can to brush against me or hold me close. It's exhilarating and exciting but at the same time it freaks me the hell out, because I like it. I *really* like it and that isn't good sign.

"Don't ever hold back what you're thinking. I like it when you say random shit." I feel the blush coat my cheeks. I clear my throat and focus back on the screens in front of me to avoid saying anything to him. I lean forward further when a live video feed with the others Dons of the family and their underbosses begins to play out. It's not them that captures my attention, it's the guy in the back who hangs in the shadows. There is something so familiar about him but I can't quite pinpoint where I know him from.

"Do you know who that is?" I ask Vin as I point to the guy. His face is hidden by the baseball cap he wears. Something in the way he holds himself and the build of his body tells me I know this man, but from where?

"No idea, Gucci, probably just one of their guys." I nod but still I can't shake this feeling I have.

"Come on, I've had enough of this and it's a beautiful day out." He pushes us back from the desk, grips my hips and lifts me while he stands. My back is flush against his chest and I have to remind myself to move and add some space between us. I've never gotten this close to a guy before. I don't let anyone aside from my family get close to me. "Get your bathing suit and let's go."

Vin and I trek through the jungle. I squeal a few times when I hit a spider web or a bug flies at me. When another bug hits me I scream. Vin reaches back, grips my hand in his and pulls me after him. Clearly he isn't happy that I'm scared of nature. I grew up in New York, we don't have a fucking jungle there or bugs the size of birds that wants to eat your face off.

Vin pushes through the big palm leaves and tugs me after him. As soon as we break through the jungle a gorgeous view hits me. There is a river that lay hidden in the middle of the jungle. I would have thought that it would be a muddy brown color or even murky given where we are but it isn't. It's clear and flowing slowly through the jungle around it. Vin drops my hand, pulls his shirt over his head, kicks his shoes off, then turns to me. The mischievous look in his eyes has me backing up a step and raising my hands.

"Don't you dare!" I warn.

"You can either take the dress off or I take you with the dress on." I search his eyes for a second and when I see he is serious, I quickly discard my dress to the side and stand before him in a yellow two-piece suite. His eyes darken as they drink in every inch of my exposed skin. Goose flesh dots my skin and I begin to burn with need. Vin doesn't even try to hide the fact he is checking me out and that is something I admire about him. He doesn't give a shit what anyone thinks. If he wants something, he goes for it and right now, he wants me. He closes the space between us until our chests are touching. This time there is no denying the sparks that are flying between us. My breathing is shallow, while his breaths are ragged as he reaches out, grips my hips and hoists me up. I wrap my arms around his neck and lock my legs around his waist. The playful look in his eyes is replaced by... hunger for me.

He shifts his hands and grips the globes of my ass as he walks us toward the water's edge. It's hot and my skin is slick but it's not just the weather that has me burning up. The way he is holding me so possessively and the raw need in his eyes has my body temperature soaring. I don't even feel the cool water as he walks us out until it's up to his chest. I dart my tongue out to moisten my suddenly dry lips. He follows the movement with his eyes. He slides one of his hands up my back until he grips the back of my neck, and searches my gaze for what, I don't know. Before I can ponder what he is thinking his grip tightens as he pulls me to him and smashes his lips against mine. I gasp. He uses my shock to his advantage and slips his tongue inside my mouth. I moan when the taste of him invades my mouth, my arms tightening around his neck, pulling him as close as I can to me.

My hands roam down his back relishing in the feel of how his muscles coil and shudder beneath my touch. I deepen the kiss and moan into his mouth as I grind down onto his hard cock. I wait for the part of my brain to kick in that always makes me panic and freak out when I touch a guy, that hasn't happened once in the time I have spent with Vin. I haven't had a single nightmare either, like he chases the bad away and keeps me safe from my own mind. He releases his hold on my neck and trails his fingers down my back until he reaches the strings of my top. I pull back. He stares into my eyes giving me every chance to back out. If I tell him to stop, he will with no questions asked and that reason alone has me nodding my head. I want him to touch me, chase away the bad memories I associate with this type of intimacy. I want him to make me feel alive and cherished even if it's just for a while.

He pulls the strings of my top and we both watch as it drops, exposing my breasts. My nipples are pebbled and aching for him to touch them. I begin to squirm in his hold as the ache between my thighs begins to worsen, he leans forward and sucks my right nipple into his mouth, electing a sharp cry from me. The warmth of his mouth and how he flicks his tongue over my nipple draws a moan from me. He switches sides and pays my other nipple the same amount of attention. He draws back and claims my lips in a searing kiss that steals the breath from my lungs. It's a kiss of owner-ship, he's marking me as his and I don't know if I should be scared or feel revered. The decision is made for me when he thrusts his hips and his cock slides against the front of my pussy, causing me to break the kiss and gasp. He licks along the side of my neck and nips at my collarbone, drawing yet another moan from me. He grips the strings on the sides of my bottoms. I stare down into his brown eyes and see lust swirling in his gaze.

"I take these off, Gucci, I'm going in." I take all of two

seconds to think on it before I'm nodding my head. "I need the words, baby."

"Vin, I-I haven't since..." I slam my mouth Closed, disgusted in myself and ashamed that I was about to voice my deepest and most depraved secret. I push away from him and quickly grab my top, and quickly secure it as I make my way toward the bank. Just as I get to waist deep water, Vin snakes and arm around my waist and hauls me back against his chest. Before I can stop it a sob tears from me and my tears begin to fall. How I could go from being so turned on and wanting him inside me, to utterly disgusted and repulsed by the idea in seconds stuns me. Vincent spins me in his arms and crushes me against his chest, saying nothing as I fall apart in his arms. For years I battled with depression and thoughts of self-harm, wanting the pain and the memories to fade, to be normal like everyone else. I never stayed at a friend's house, never hung out with guys aside from my brothers, too scared they would use my body to satisfy their own sick fucking wants. I watched my friends happily pack to go home to their families over the break, while I dreaded returning to that fucking house, the house that holds so many dark memories. I never sleep while I'm there–I can't. Every time I close my eyes all I see is him coming into my room every night, setting up his tri pod and recording me. Recording what he did to his five-year-old fucking daughter!

Chapter Thirteen

Vincent

I sit on the recliner with my arms hanging between my legs, staring at her asleep on the bed. The soft glow of the bedside lamp allows me to see the strain in her features. She broke down today and was inconsolable. I carried her the whole way back as she clung to me begging me not to leave her. I whispered sweet nothings in her ear even though it killed me to not be the one that ended Tony-fuck-ing-Murdoch. The things I would have done to that cunt for how he hurt her would make even *The Godfather* cringe. She tosses in her sleep, frown lines marking her angelic face and I just know she is having a nightmare. If she didn't have a panic attack today, I would have crossed a line with her that I could never come back from. The princess of the Murdoch family has woven her way into my bloodstream and I don't know if I can get her out—do I want her out?

"Please... no, stop!" she shouts in her sleep. Before I know what I'm doing, I'm on my feet and eliminating the distance between us. I kneel down beside the bed and brush her wayward strands of hair from her face, noticing then that her skin is clammy. I cup her face between my hands.

"Gucci?" I try the gentle approach but when she begins to whimper and thrash in my hold, I shake her awake. Her eyes snap open. They are unfocused and wide with fear until they land on me. A breath escapes her then her eyes begin to lose the scared look in them. I see the terrified little girl in her eyes and a pang hits me in the chest. Is that how Selena looked when our father sold her to the Murdoch's?

"Vin?" I shake my head and push that thought away as I focus back on her. I try to smile reassuringly but from the look of apprehension on her face, I know I failed. "Are you okay?" The fact that she is the one trying to comfort me right now has a small laugh escaping me. This girl is an oddity, that is for sure.

"I should be asking you that question." A sad smile graces her face but even I can see it's forced. A deep resigned sigh escapes her. She drops her eyes from mine, I won't have that so I reach out and grip her chin, lifting it until her beautiful brown eyes are on mine.

"I'm okay," she whispers.

"How often do you have these nightmares?" Since the night I met her she has only had nightmares twice, and call me crazy, but both times have been when I'm not lying next to her.

"Every night until... recently," she admits. I keep my expression neutral not wanting to give away my thoughts.

"Want to talk about it?" I offer a moment of silence. She

eyes me warily, then pulls out of my hold and shifts into a sitting position. I slowly rise to my feet now, allowing her to have the more dominant position for this conversation.

"You have a fucking file on me, go read it and you'll have your answer." The anger in her voice isn't directed at me, it's at herself. The fire in her eyes shows me she will fight me tooth and nail the whole way. Good, Gucci, because I love a challenge.

"Is that what you want, you want me to read about it instead of you telling me?" I'm bluffing. I don't have shit in that file aside from the basic shit that I have told her about. Her face contorts in rage before she slips from the bed and stands in front of me. I expect her to shout, scream or stomp her foot. What I don't fucking expect is for her to *slap* me! My head snaps to the side and I stay like that for a moment until the shock wears off and I slowly turn back to face her, anger simmering in my veins that she would have the nerve to strike me!

"You're a bastard. You kidnap me and expect me to sit here and spill all my secrets so you can use that shit against me and my family." She scoffs and doesn't even give me a chance to defend myself before continuing to berate me. "You think you are so much better than me and my brothers. Newsflash, asshole, you're not! You are exactly like us. You are no better than Bishop. You thrive off the feeling of being in control. You need control in order to function. You love to hunt your prey. I see it every day in your eyes when you watch me." The unfiltered hatred that I see in her eyes has the small ember inside me catching alight and burning bright in her presence. This girl is everything and she isn't scared of me, which is refreshing. She strikes out to hit me again. This time I catch her wrist and move us so fast she has no time to prepare. She is flat on her back on the bed with me on top of her, pinning her arms above her.

"No one lays a fucking hand on me," I snarl right in her face. She doesn't cower or shrink back into the bed. She lifts her head so our noses touch, her upper lip is pulled back baring her teeth.

"Well, clearly I'm not no one. I am Carlina Murdoch and I make what my brothers do look like a kid's carnival. I will destroy you worse than any of them ever could, Vincent. I will be your demise, if you don't fucking let me go!" she screams the last part right in my face.

"You want to ruin me because I asked you about your daddy, but me kidnapping you turns you the fuck on to the point you wanted my cock inside you hours ago?" Her eyes widen in shock. She thrashes beneath me but I don't even budge. She is latching onto her anger and lashing out at me because she would rather that, than admit her darkest secret. Something inside me tells me Carlina has never told anyone the truth about what happened to her. She may have allowed them to draw their own conclusions but never admitted the truth fully.

"You're disgusting. I would never let that needle dick God cursed you to walk the earth with inside me. You disgust me. You are beneath me and I would never sully myself or my family by fucking the likes of you!"

Fuck that... hurt. I didn't expect her words to hit me that hard but fuck did they ever. I flick my eyes between hers, searching for what? I have no fucking idea. I guess the part of me that is willing to bend my own rules and throw them out the window is trying to spot if she is lying. No, fuck that, I know she is lying. There is no way she was faking her reaction to me today. I could see the raw unfiltered need in her eyes. I leap from her as if she burnt me. Her shocked eyes scan me up and down, waiting to see what I will do next, but the truth is, I don't know what I am doing. When it comes to her, I have no fucking idea what I am meant to be doing or what I am going to do. She is a fucking mind fuck! She scrambles from the bed closing the space I put between us and then begins to wail on my chest, punching and slapping me. I stand here stunned for a minute wondering what the fuck is going on.

"Hit me. Don't be a pussy, fucking do something." Sobs tear from her. Her tiny frame begins to quake with tremors as she cries. Her hits become sluggish and that snaps me out of it. I smack her hands out of the way, then wrap my arms around her and crush her against my chest. She fights me with all she has but I won't budge. A few seconds pass before her tiny arms wrap around me and she fucking breaks out into gut wrenching sobs that have me slamming my eyes closed to try control my own emotions from breaking free. We stand like this for so long, me just holding her while she breaks down in my arms, then I carefully lift her into my arms as she wraps around me like a monkey and I move us toward the bed. I maneuver us until my back rests against the headboard with her straddling me and resting her head in the crook of my neck. Time seems to still as we stay in this position for so long that I begin to get cramps in my arms from holding her against me so tightly. She's not crying anymore and the fact she has been laying against me for so long silently has me nervous. I know she isn't asleep as she will sigh or shift and for the past few minutes she has been shifting around. I am trying everything I can to will my cock to remain flaccid and not get hard, easier said than done.

"I didn't mean it, I shouldn't have said those horrid

things I did." I place a kiss to the top of her head and tighten my hold on her.

"I know, Gucci—"

"You don't though. I'm a job to you, someone you can use to take down my brother. I'm not stupid, Vincent. I know you want to watch my family burn to the ground because you think they wronged you, but I can't allow that to happen no matter how I feel."

"And how exactly do you feel?"

"I think I made my feelings pretty obvious today." I fight the smug smile that wants to break free.

"Then why did you freak out?"

"You gonna put this in your file if I tell you?"

"No." The thought never crossed my mind and even if it did, I could never betray her or hurt her like that. I know that what she is about to say is going to rock the foundation which I view her on.

Chapter Fourteen

Carlina

I am putting blind trust into Vincent here but I need to tell someone. I'm suffocating and slowly losing my soul to the devil. Tony Murdoch corrupted me and used me for his own sick gain. He never cared about how he hurt me or how it made me feel each time he would come into my room. In the short amount of time I have been with Vin, I feel like he could understand me, almost like he has been through the same thing as I have. He doesn't look at me with pity or disgust. He doesn't touch my body like it repulses him, but like I am delicate and everything. He has no idea how his touch has me healing and now I see myself in a different light.

"Tony, my own father, used me like a toy. Well not my mind, just my body." I feel Vin tense beneath me but I know if I stop now, I won't be able to ever tell him again. He needs to know why I freaked out today. I want him to know. "I was five when it first started. He said we were having daddy daughter time because I needed to know I was so special to him. I loved that idea as he always spent so much time with my brothers and never any with me. I was so stupid. Bishop and King were off doing as they were told to prove they could be worthy. I was stuck at home playing mommy to the twins, that's why the three of us are so close."

"He used the twins against you, didn't he?" His voice is rough and laced with anger.

"Not at first. When I was younger, he didn't have to do anything. He could just overpower me and threaten to hurt me to keep me quiet. He used the twins against me when he started doing the same thing to my friend that he was to me. I couldn't allow my brothers to suffer through what I went through every night. Anytime I would try to resist him or object to him videoing me or... what he did to me, he would threaten to bring Rook in and make him watch." The thought of my brothers seeing what happened to me makes my stomach roll and bile threatening to spill out of me. "Tony broke a part of me I will never be able to repair. He stole my innocence and robbed me of a childhood, used my love for my brothers against me and it nearly killed me! It was the best day of my fucking life, the day he died. It was the first time I actually felt free and happy."

"Today in the water—"

"I got triggered and it caused me to freak out. I haven't... I've never been with anyone by choice."

"You're still a virgin?" I snort, was he not listening to what the fuck I just said?

"I just told you—"

"Fuck that!" The anger that laces his tone has me clamping my mouth closed. "That doesn't count. A woman's virginity is a gift. You did not give it willingly, so it doesn't fucking count. Do you hear me, Gucci?" I push back from him and rest my hands against his chest as I stare into his eyes. I can tell from the hardened look on his face he means what he says.

"You really mean that, don't you?" I whisper in shock, out of everything I said he hasn't shoved me off him. He doesn't look disgusted by me and the lustful look that is always in his eyes when he looks at me is still there. He leans forward and cups my face between his hands, stroking his thumbs against my cheeks.

"Carlina, what happened to you wasn't your fault. Mothers and fathers are supposed to protect their children, not destroy them. I am so sorry I wasn't there to watch your brother put a bullet between his fucking eyes." My mouth drops open in shock, a small chuckle escapes him before he continues. "I know everything, Gucci. I also know there is a Russian girl tailing your brother's girl right now. Prove to me you are good girl and can listen and I might even let you send them a warning." I'm stunned by his answer and unsure what the hell I am supposed to say to that? He leans in until our foreheads are touching. His eyes bore into mine and the look of need and longing in his gaze robs my lungs of air. "You are no victim, Gucci. You are a fucking survivor. What happened in your past does not define who you are. You can choose to let it consume you or fight for your right to live and say I survived that shit and I'm stronger than ever."

His words have tears clouding my vision and a lump forming in my throat. Never did I ever think someone would come along and understand how I have felt or even take the time to help me process my nightmare. Without thinking, I smash my lips against his and pour all of my gratitude and want into this kiss. I need him to help me forget and replace Tony's unwanted touch with his needed touch. I want him—no need him to make sex something other than torture and painful memories for me. He is the first man to know exactly who I am and not give a shit about it. He can lie and say that he will kill me but I can see it in his eyes every time he looks at me, he would never hurt me. I deepen the kiss and run my fingers through his hair, then tug on the strands. He moans into my mouth. I grind down onto his growing erection and relish in the hiss that escapes him. When he grips my hips and slams me down onto his now hard cock I gasp into his mouth.

Vin grips the ends of my shirt and pulls it up. I break our kiss to help him rid me of my shirt. Before I can reclaim his lips, he ducks his head and latches onto my nipple electing a strangled moan from me. He swirls his tongue around my nipple whilst using his other hand to twirl my left nipple between his fingers. I throw my head back and moan as I grind down against his cock. He releases my nipple with a pop and grips the back of my neck and pulls my face down until his mouth is on mine. I continue to grind against his cock and love the moans that tumble from him. It's an exhilarating feeling knowing that I am the one bringing this big man this amount of pleasure. I run my hands down his naked chest and practically purr when he shudders beneath my touch. He breaks the kiss, both of us are panting and trying to catch our breath.

"Are you sure you want to do this?" It's not the question, it's the fact that he was thoughtful enough to be concerned about me enough to not think with his cock, that has me nodding my head. He lifts me and rolls us so I am beneath him, leans back and rests on his haunches gazing down at me. It may sound shallow but I'm proud of my body. All the years of cheering has made sure my body is in tip top shape. "Fuck, you are beautiful." I feel the blush creep all the way from my chest to my neck, and finally my face. "Last chance, Gucci. I need to be inside you now."

"You kidnapped me, held me against my will and threatened to kill me more times than I can count and yet now, you give me the option to have a say?" I meant it as a joke but he frowns and I see his eyes flick from mine. I know he is battling within himself so I reach down and begin to push my sleep shorts down. It takes half a second before he takes over and rips them from my body. His eyes spark with lust as he peers down at my naked pussy. He darts his tongue out to moisten his lips, the intensity of his gaze has me squirming beneath him and an ache forming at my core.

"Just one taste." His words aren't meant for me. He moves off the bed kneeling down beside it, grips my ankles and yanks me down. I push up on my elbows ready to ask what he is doing but the words die in my mouth when he buries his face between my legs and eats my soaking wet pussy. The feeling of his tongue swiping through my folds and the groan that tumbles from his sinful mouth has me moaning. This is a first for me, I've never been eaten out before. He flicks his eyes to me and by God if this isn't the sexiest moment of my life. His tongue pushes inside my tight, wet hole while he keeps his needy gaze on me the whole time. Fuck, just the way he is looking at me like I am his last meal has me hot and needy for him.

Chapter Fifteen

Vincent

She bucks against my face and her cries grow louder, while a sheen of sweat coats her body telling me she is close to coming all over my face. I slip a finger inside her wet cunt and growl my approval. She is fucking soaking wet and so ready for me to slip my aching cock inside her. I flatten my tongue against her clit as I pump my finger in and out of her at a brutal pace. She screams my name as she shatters beneath me, her body trembling as I place kisses to her inner thighs, letting her come down slowly. I slowly pull my finger out and rise to my feet. Her hazy eyes track my movements. I make sure to hold her gaze as I bring my finger to my mouth and suck it clean. Her mouth opens slightly, pupils dilating with lust. The taste of her on my tongue has my cock aching in my shorts, begging for me to bury myself balls deep inside her pussy.

I push my shorts and boxers down. My cock springs free and smacks against my stomach. I grip the base of my cock in my hand and pump it. A heady moan escapes her as she sits up on the bed and scoots forward so her face is level with my cock. Her gaze flicks to mine as she reaches out, smacks my hand away, then replaces it with her dainty little one. A hiss escapes me. Having her hands on my cock has a shudder rolling through me. She pulls her gaze from mine to stare at my cock as she pumps it a few times causing me to stiffen and fight the urge to come all over her face like a fucking teen boy.

"Stop teasing, Gucci. Suck it or lay the fuck back so I can fuck the shit out of you." Her defiant gaze meets mine. My breath hitches at the cunning look in her eyes as she darts her tongue out and swipes it across the head of my dick. I throw my head back and groan. She sucks my cock into her mouth and the wet hot heat of her mouth wrapped around my cock has my balls tightening. I grip the back of her head and wrap her hair around my hand. I wait a few seconds to see if she will freak out, when she doesn't, I tighten my hold and take over. I thrust my hips, fucking her face. She deep throats my cock like a pro. My girl has no gag reflex and fuck if that shit doesn't make me hotter for her. "That's it, baby, swallow my cock like a good girl." She moans and the vibration has me yanking my dick out before I really do come down her throat. She sits here panting and trying to catch her breath. Spit drips down her chin and I follow the trail as it glides down her perfect full tits.

"Stop staring and touch them." She has no qualms in voicing what she wants and I fucking love that. I oblige her and push backward. She scoots up the bed and I crawl on top of her. I lick a trail from the top of her pussy to her tits, then suck her nipple into my mouth. Her back arches off the bed and she cries out. She locks her legs around my waist and tries to use them to pull me to her. I hold fast and switch to the other nipple paying it the same amount of attention. By the time I am finished, she is a writhing panting mess. I capture her lips in a kiss of ownership. She wraps her arms around my neck but I break free of her hold and pull back to stare down at her. "What's wrong?"

"I put my cock inside you, Gucci, you're mine. Do you understand?" It's probably a dick move on my part asking her this when she is strung out and so fucking turned on but I never said I was good man. I'll do whatever I have to, to keep Carlina. I don't wait for a reply, I don't need to. The look in her eyes tells me she knows her fate is sealed. She is mine to do with as I please. I line my cock up to her entrance and hold her gaze as I slowly push inside her. She's so fucking tight it's almost painful, but fuck it feels so good. Her face is contorted in pain, if I was a better man I would pull out and whisper words of love but I'm not. I don't want to drag this out so I slam the rest of the way inside her. She arches off the bed screaming in pain and fuck the sound of her pain has my cock aching.

"Vin..." she cries out, tears drip down her cheeks. I lean down and lick them, loving the taste of her tears. "It hurts."

"I know, baby. I'm gonna make you feel so good." She nods. I kiss her as I start to move inside her. Her body is stiff and tense but within seconds of me moving inside her, she relaxes, her whimpers turn to moans, her death grip on my arms moves to my back as she scrapes her nails down my spine causing me to shudder. I feel her pussy begin to clench my cock and know she is close. I pull out of her. She opens her mouth to protest but clamps it closed when I lift her off the bed. She locks her arms and legs around me before claiming my lips. I spin us away from the bed and don't stop until she is against the wall. I break the kiss, grip the globes of her ass and push her up my body until her legs are over my shoulders and her dripping pussy is right in my face.

"Vin, what are—Oh fuck!" she screams out when I suck her clit into my mouth. She grips my hair in her hand, holding my face steady as she grinds her pussy against my face. The scent and taste of her overwhelms my senses and fuck if it isn't the best sensory overload I have ever had. "Just like that, Vin. Fuck. Yes. Make me come!" she screams out. I push my tongue inside her and love the sounds she makes as I tongue fuck her cunt. Within seconds she is screaming out her release, this time I don't give her time to ride out her aftershocks. I lower her limp body down until she is impaled on my cock. "Fuck!" she cries out when my dick is balls deep inside her cunt. Her pussy walls are clenching the fuck out of my cock. I fuck her at a savage pace chasing my own release. She locks her arms around my neck and kisses me while I continue to thrust inside her.

I break the kiss and suck on her neck, needing to leave my brand on her skin. My balls begin to tighten and I know I am seconds out from coming deep inside her. I try to pull out knowing I haven't gloved up but she locks her legs around me holding me in place.

"Come inside me, but make me come on your cock first." Fuck, this girl is perfect. I won't last long enough to make her come with just my cock so I reach between us and pinch her clit between my thumb and index fingers. She cries out exploding all over my cock, I follow after her roaring my release as I spill everything I have inside her.

I'm startled awake to the feeling of her lips wrapped around my cock. I smile up at the ceiling before I lift the blanket and peer down at her. I throw the blanket off and reach down to move her hair from her face. The sight of her bobbing up and down on my cock has a moan tumbling from my lips. I thrust my hips up needing her to take me deeper, and growl when she releases my cock with a wet pop and smiles up at me like she is fucking innocent.

"You best be finishing what you just..." My words trail off when she shuffles up the bed spins around, and climbs on top of me so we can sixty-fucking-nine. She sucks my cock back into her mouth as she lowers her pussy to my mouth. I reach up and grip her ass cheeks in the palms of my hands pulling her down until she's sitting right on my fucking face. Neither of us draw this out needing the release. I feel my balls tightening and know I'm seconds away from coming. I tap her ass a couple times letting her know. She ignores me and sucks my cock all the way into the back of her throat, making me come instantly, moaning her name against her pussy. She swallows every fucking drop of cum and fuck if that isn't the sexiest fucking thing. A woman willing to swallow, I hit the jackpot with her. She licks me clean, then sits up, climbs off me, only to turn around so she is facing the other way and sits right on my fucking face. She grinds her pussy against my face moaning my name. I reach up and cup her tits, loving the needy moan that spills from her.

"Just like that, make me come all over your fucking face, Vin." Her wish is my command. A minute later she is screaming out her release. I lap at her pussy letting her ride out the aftershocks of her orgasm. I could wake up like this every fucking morning and be the happiest man alive.

Chapter Sixteen

Carlina

Six weeks....

"What are they planning?" I stir awake to the sound of Vin's raised voice. I blink my eyes open and find it is still dark out. Vin is sitting at his desk with his phone to his ear and his monitors in front of him. For the past two weeks he has been doing this, something is up and I know he is hiding shit from me. "Find out how the fuck they are keeping this operation running without Tony in the picture." At the mention of my father's name I sit up and gasp. Vin spins around to face me. He mutters a curse beneath his breath before telling whoever is on the phone he'll call them back. He drops his phone to his desk, then he's sitting on the edge of the bed cupping my face between his hands. I search his eyes trying to figure out what the hell is going on. "How much of that did you hear?"

I shake my head. "Not much, why are you talking about Tony?" I plead with my eyes for him to not lie to me. We have had the most amazing time together these past weeks. He has taken me out exploring and dancing, shown me a completely different side of him. Our outings have stopped since he said we had a tail, we don't know if one of my brother's men or someone else. Vin said he wasn't taking any chances so he has locked us down here at his house. So instead, Vin has taken to training me to fight and teaching me to track. It's a lot harder to track someone than I thought.

"How much do you know about the other families, Gucci?" I furrow my brow in confusion.

"Not a lot. Bishop doesn't tell me anything about that stuff." An angry glint enters his gaze. Whenever I mention my brothers, Vin always gets an angry look in his eyes and I don't understand why!

"He done you a disservice by keeping you in the dark." I open my mouth to defend my brother but he pushes on. "You need to know about these things so you are not ever put in danger." I snort.

"Well, if that was the case, I wouldn't have ended up here with *you*." He narrows his eyes and growls which just causes me to smirk.

"Smartass. Look, the other families are making a move against yours."

"Why?"

"Your brother has shut down the skin trade and they are losing millions a year because of him, they need that trade in order to keep making money. They want your brother out so he doesn't cause problems between them and the Russian's." I mull over his words letting them sink in for a moment before I answer.

"What are you trying to do here, Vincent?" He rolls his lips over his teeth. I can see it in his eyes, he wants to lie but he swore to me that he is many things but not a liar. He scrubs a hand down his and releases a whoosh of air, his shoulders are tense.

"You won't like the truth, Gucci." His tone is void of emotion, it worries me sometimes how he can detach from his emotions so easily. Will he be able to turn his feelings for me off so easily?

"I need to know, Vin... please."

"I'm supposed to be dead." My eyes widen in surprise but I remain silent so he will continue. "My father is Vinny Murelo and I hate that son of a bitch more than I hate your father." I can feel the tension and anger radiating off of him. "I faked my own death to get away from my family and all the others, it was the only way I would be able to do what I do now."

"What happened, why did you... fake your death?" A sad smile spreads across his face.

"As cliché as it sounds, it was all over a girl." My face falls, my chest cracks and an unwanted feeling of jealousy spikes inside me. One stupid girl managed to change the course of Vin's life.

"She sounds peachy," I spit out, darting my gaze away from him, unable to bring myself to stare into his eyes while he pictures his lost love. He grips my chin and pulls my gaze back to his. I narrow my eyes in warning, not giving a shit that he looks pissed off.

"Jealousy looks good on you, Gucci."

"Fuck you."

"Not right now."

"It's not happening again," I sass back.

"The girl was my sister, Carlina." *Oh shit!* I feel like an utter bitch now. Here I am moping because I thought Vin had fallen in love with a girl and that girl wasn't me. "My piece of shit father sold her to Tony, who then sold her to the Russian's I believe as a goodwill payment." Anger burns through me, it makes me sick that men think they can sell women off like we are nothing but chattel. "I couldn't do anything to help her under Vinny's rule so with the help of my cousin Marco, we faked a car wreck and placed a John Doe in the driver's seat before burning the car. We knew Vinny would never check dental records, he never gave a shit about me or Selena. He was just happy to get rid of us."

"So all of this," I wave my hands around the room to emphasize my point, "is to find out what happened to your sister?"

"Yes."

"You came for me as a bargaining chip to get to Bishop so he would help you find your sister, didn't you?" He runs a hand through his hair tugging on the strands in frustration. A whoosh of air escapes me as realization dawns on me. "You were going to use me and then kill me so Bish could feel half the pain you feel right now." A pained look enters his eyes. I pull out of his hold and shuffle away from him. He tries to reach for me but I dodge him and jump from the bed, keeping it between us as a barrier.

"Gucci—"

"Fuck you, Vincent! You used me and are still doing it now. Did you send videos of you fucking me to my brother?" His eyes widen for a split second before he's jumping over the bed and crowding me against the wall. His hand comes up to wrap around my throat. His hold isn't tight enough to restrict my airways, the hold he has on me is just a warning that he could do it if he wanted to.

"The only one who gets to see this," he cups my sex, causing me to gasp, "is me. Make no fucking mistake, Gucci, I told you from the start I had planned to kill you. I'll find another way to get what I want from your brother but it won't be at the cost of you." I'm so fucked in the head, instead of his words inspiring a deep-seated hate for him admitting to going after my family, they have me feeling all warm inside because he won't use me to get what he wants most. "My intentions were clear from the start. You knew you were going to be used but I didn't expect for shit to change and you to bury your fucking self inside me. I need to find my sister, Carlina. I have to. But I promise you, I would *never* betray you by using our most private moments to get what I want. I am the only man who gets to see you come on my cock. No one else will ever see the face you make in that moment. Am I clear?"

"Y-yeah," I stutter.

"Good." He places a quick peck to my lips before he pulls back and leads me back to the bed. "Go back to sleep, Gucci. I have some work to do and we leave for Paris in two days."

"Wait, what?" A devilish smirk graces his handsome face.

"You see, I kind of don't get paid from my previous job because you're still breathing so I need to work." Like I said, I'm so fucked up because I swoon like he just said the most romantic shit ever.

Seven weeks...

Weeks have gone by and we have traveled to more places than I thought possible. Vin's work takes him all over the world. I expected him to leave me behind and not want me with him, but Vincent was not having any of that. I travel with him under a fake name and passport. I even wear wigs to hide my hair color. I stay in the hotel room while he *works*. It's surreal to know that he is leaving me to go kill someone. I've read over every file and each person that he is sent to take out isn't a good man. They harm children and women, steal from the poor and Vin assures me he never takes a life unless it is warranted. He says he needs all the facts about a person before he pulls the trigger. He is very thorough with his checks and never rushes.

We have been home for two days. Vin has given me my freedom and phone back while we were in Sicily saying that if I chose to out him and call in my brothers, that it's my choice. The thought never crossed my mind, we may have started out fucked up, but honestly I care a lot about Vin. My feelings for him seem to grow stronger and stronger each passing day. I would even dare to go as far and say I've fallen in love with him. The only thing that scares me is knowing I will have to come clean to my family and tell them about him. Vin is older than Bishop, he's thirty-one, and is the only son of my brother's enemy. Bishop is not going to take that well.

Vin gave me a file the night we came home on a woman named Koby. He has been tracking each person in my family for years. He says he may live like a recluse but he has contacts around the world and each of them report to him about what they find on my family and all their dealings. This woman Koby is a Russian and she is trying to get in close with Allison, King's girlfriend. I know I need to warn my brothers about her but I don't know how Vin is going to feel about that. He has some app on my phone that blocks it from being able to be tracked or bugged. Yeah, Vin knows about Luka and his hacking skills. He has opened up so much and told me everything about himself and his sister Selena, my heart aches for him. I wouldn't be able to survive losing one of my siblings, shit, even losing Gage would hurt like a bitch.

Chapter Seventeen

Vincent

Present... the day Knight called.

We're sitting on the couch with her laying her head on my lap while I run my fingers through her hair. I love the feeling of her silky strands as they fall through my fingers. Spending these past months with her has been the best of my life. She has given me a whole new outlook on life. I never thought I would wake each day with a smile on my face and be happy to wake up, knowing she is beside me every morning makes me fucking happy to be alive. Her phone rings pulling me from my thoughts. She reaches blindly toward the coffee table to grab it. When she sees the caller ID she bolts upright and darts her gaze to me. I grit my teeth and remind myself that she is no longer my prisoner and is staying with me by choice. Even if she wanted to leave I don't think I would ever be able to let her go. Carlina Murdoch was once my enemy but now she is my... everything.

"Knight," she breathes his name out almost like it's painful. I'm close enough to her to hear what he says without it being on speaker.

"Hey, Car." The tension in her shoulders eases slightly.

"How did you find me?" I smile wide, I'm proud of my girl. She has changed so much and isn't naïve to the things she used to be. She can fight and track me through the jungle without getting lost. Truth is, she is just as good as me at tracking and that is saying something. I didn't earn the name bloodhound for nothing.

"There's a lot to fill you in on but first, I need you to come home." Tension returns to her shoulders, she drops her chin to her chest and rage burns inside me knowing that her brother has made her feel this way.

"I was wondering how long it would take before one of you guys came calling. Truthfully, I expected you lot to get Rook to guilt me into coming back willingly." She's told me about all her brothers and how each of their relationships differs. Out of the five of them, she is closest to her youngest brother, Rook.

"Car... Rook is..." She snaps her gaze to me, the scared look in her eyes spears right in the fucking heart knowing I can't make it better.

"What the fuck is going on, Knight. Where is he?" The concern in her voice for her brother is felt deep inside me. Without a doubt I know she will want to go back if something happened to him. Honestly, I've been putting off this trip for so long. This might just be the push I needed to finally end this with my father and her family.

"There was an... accident and he——"

"Don't fucking say it!" she pleads, the watery tone of her voice lets me know she is close to tears. I wrap my arm around her shoulders and pull her into my side, placing a kiss to the top of her head.

"He's missing, we need you to come home now. We're at war and Bishop won't make a move until we know you are here safe." She looks up at me pleading with her eyes to give her strength. I give her a curt nod letting her know I will follow her home.

"I'll be back as soon as I can... Knight?"

"Yeah?"

"I want to know everything when I get back, don't water shit down for me." She makes me so fucking proud. Her brothers are going to be in for the shock of their lives when they learn she won't let them just walk all over her.

"Deal. When you're back, I want an explanation about how you knew about Koby and Dimitri."

"Okay, just... promise to keep an open mind." I can picture her brother on the other end of the phone trying to tamper his rage at the fact she won't just blurt out what he wants to know.

"Okay." She promises to be back within the week before ending the call. She places her phone on the table before turning back to me. She nibbles on her bottom lip which I have come to learn is a nervous gesture. I don't coddle her like she is used to, she needs to find the strength within herself to say whatever it is she needs to.

"I need to go home, my family needs me."

"Okay." Her eyes widen in surprise at my response.

"Seriously? You're not going to say no and shout and say you'll kill me if I leave?" I shake my head and smile at her.

"No, I'm coming with you." Tears cloud her vision.

"You would do that for me?" I release a loud exhale and decide to give her the whole story.

"Truth is, I have been planning on returning to the states for a while. I put it off because I know what I have to do is going to hurt you. I never want to hurt you, Carlina, and I fucking hate myself for how I treated you that first day here. I had no fucking right to put my hands on you—" She doesn't allow me to finish as she launches herself at me and straddles my lap before smashing her lips against mine. This girl has no fucking idea that I would burn every single one of her enemies alive for even thinking they could ever hurt her. Carlina Murdoch has quickly become something I won't—no, can't live without. She pulls back and smiles down at me and fuck me if that isn't the most beautiful sight I have ever seen.

"I need you to promise me something." Here it is.

"I know what you are going to ask me and I can't promise you that. Your brothers are going to come for me, Gucci, and I'm no pussy. I won't let them fuck me raw without a fight, they need to learn that no matter what you belong to me."

"I know." I furrow my brows at her, fucking confused.

"You know what?" She rolls her eyes playfully.

"Vincent, you are as much mine as I am yours. If any women tries to touch what is mine I'll slit her throat and hide her body in the backyard." Hearing how possessive she is of me has my cock growing hard beneath her. I fucking love it when she talks about murder.

"I'm gonna fuck you now," I say as I lean forward to capture her lips. She places her hand against my chest and pushes me back earning herself a growl from me.

"Promise me you will at least try with my brothers... tell them who you *really* are and *why* you are doing this. Bishop isn't Tony." I search her gaze for what I have no fucking idea but the thought of ever being near her brother and not killing him has me wanting to laugh. But for her, I have to try. She is the only fucking person in this world that would be able to get me to agree to something like this.

"Fine."

"Thank you."

"I'm not done." She tenses and her eyes narrow. "If he doesn't give me the information I need or tries anything, he goes down."

"You are not killing my fucking brother!"

"Fine, he can live but you and me are leaving and if he so much as tries to stop you, Gucci, or take you away from me, I will fucking kill him where he stands. You belong to me!" This woman is going to be the fucking death of me. She bites her lip and moans as she grinds down on my cock drawing a hiss from me.

"You say the most sexy, fucking things. Now, fuck me so we can pack and go home." I lean forward and suck on her neck drawing a needy moan from her. I love leaving my mark on her for every fucker to see she belongs to me!

"Get on the fucking bed, Gucci. I think you need a reminder of who this fucking pussy belongs to."

Chapter Eighteen

Carlina

Two days later...

I'm a ball of freaking nerves as Vin and I board the plane. He booked us first class tickets. We couldn't leave straight away as he said he had to ship the gear he would need to take out his father and Pauly privately. I have no idea what that means and I honestly didn't care. I was saddened to leave our little hut. I never thought I would say this but I loved being out in the jungle with no noise or people around, just me and Vin out there alone with nothing but each other's company. I made Vin promise that he would bring me back to our hut. He swore that he would. I know he hates the city and I have to admit I'm not looking forward to going back to all the hustle and bustle. I'm excited as hell to see my family but scared at the same time. Bishop and King are going to lose their shit. Vin said to use my real passport because he and I both know Luka will be hacking the video feeds at JFK.

I claim my seat as Vin places our bags in the overhead compartment. Our seats are next to each other but we are not close, it's like we have our own little cubicles. Our seats stretch out to make a bed, even doors we can close for privacy. Vin drops into his seat and shoots me a wink before buckling up. I grab my phone and check it for the hundredth time, I have so many missed messages from Kiara but after a while I stopped replying. I didn't need to check in, I'm a grown ass woman and can live my own life. Vin and I haven't been able to keep our hands off each other since Knight called, were both avoiding addressing the problem. We have no idea at the end of this if we will be together or if the man I have fallen in love with will die at the hands of my family. The thought alone has tears springing to my eyes. I can't lose Vin, he has helped me more than anyone. He has made me see I am beautiful, I'm not damaged or broken. He's made me a sex crazed woman. I hated the thought of sex until Vin, now I'm the one that is jumping him any chance I can get. I love the feeling of having him inside me.

Fuck, I'm wet just thinking about him inside me. I wait for the plane to take off, then unbuckle my seatbelt. I turn to Vin and reach over to push the lid of his laptop closed. He looks to me in confusion as I slink back into my seat and slowly recline my chair so it's now the size of a small single bed. His gaze remains on me the whole time, still not getting what I'm selling so I pop the button on my jeans and hold his stare as I mouth the words, *I need you.*

Vin is out of his seat and jumping into my little cubicle.

He pushes the button to close the door, then he's unbuck-
ling his jeans as I'm pushing mine down. When my jeans
hit the floor, he reaches down, grips my soaked yellow
thong, brings it to his nose and inhales. The sight of him
sniffing my thong has me clenching my thighs closed to try
and dull the ache.

"Fuck, your pussy smells so good, Gucci." I open my
legs to bare my dripping wet cunt to him, making him dart
his tongue out, moistening his lips.

"I taste even better, big man." He doesn't need to be told
twice. He rids himself of his shirt, chucks it at me then
lowers to his knees.

"Bite down on that and don't make a fucking sound or
you don't come." I nod my head eagerly and do as he says
balling the shirt up and shoving it in my mouth as he dips
his head between my legs and fucking feasts on my pussy
like a starved man. Vin is not a selfish lover, he loves to get
me off before himself and makes sure each time we have sex
that I am always the first to come. He sucks my clit into his
mouth and I bite down on the shirt to keep myself from
screaming out. I don't know why I thought I could be quiet,
I'm never quiet when it comes to Vin ravishing my body.

"Hmmm," I moan into the shirt trying so fucking hard
to be quiet, but it's hard when he is making me see stars. I
thrust my hips up grind my pussy against his face. He grips
my ass cheeks and holds me in place as he continues to suck
and lick the fuck out of my pussy. I reach down and lift my
shirt, pull the cups of my bra down and twirl my nipples
making me arch my back. I feel my pending orgasm cresting
and grind against his face faster chasing it. Right as I'm
about to shatter, he stops. I spit the shirt out of my mouth
and glare at him as he slowly climbs to his feet. "What the
hell?" I whisper shout. He smirks down at me before

nestling himself between my legs, lining his cock up with my entrance as he speaks.

"You're going to be coming on my cock, not my face. Now keep fucking quiet or you'll be sucking me off and remain on edge for the rest of the flight." I balk at him. He cannot be fucking serious? Before I can ask, he clamps a hand over my mouth and slams inside me. I cry out, his hand only muffles my sounds slightly. If someone were to walk past, they would know exactly what we are doing in here and I can't find it within myself to care. I need Vin to make me come. I need this orgasm to help relieve the stress of seeing my family again for the first time in months. He bends down and sucks the flesh of my neck into his mouth. I fucking love when he does this. He groans as my pussy clenches his cock, my orgasm is right there. He replaces his hand with his mouth and swallows my cries as I come all over his cock like he wanted. His pace doesn't slow, it picks up as he chases his own release and moans into my mouth as he comes deep inside me.

We both lay here panting with his head buried in the crook of my neck, our bodies are slick with sweat and I know my hair must be a mess but I don't care. I needed that. Vin rests up on his elbows and peers down at me with a lazy smile on his handsome face. Vincent has no idea how devastatingly handsome he is.

"I love you," I blurt out. He freezes above me and his eyes widen to the size of dinner plates. I wish the ground would open up and swallow me fucking whole, I'm such an idiot for saying that out loud. Tears build behind my eyes as shame washes over me. I turn my head unable to look at him and know he doesn't feel the same way about me. The first tear falls as he cups my cheek gently and turns me back to face him. I slam my eyes closed not wanting to look at him as he tells me he doesn't feel the way I feel.

"Open your eyes, Gucci." I shake my head. "Baby, my cock is still inside you." The reminder of that has me snapping my eyes open and glaring up at him.

"Get the fuck out of me!" I grit out through clenched teeth. A cunning smirk crosses his face.

"Never."

"I don't want you."

"Don't lie, you want me more than you want to breathe and I want you just as much." I scoff.

"You're so full of shit, that's why your eyes are brown." His eyes harden as he leans down until our foreheads touch. The intensity of his gaze sears me and it fucking hurts. I want him to want me.

"I love you too, Carlina. If I didn't, I wouldn't be on this fucking plane right now with you joining the mile high club." My mouth drops open, taken back by his words.

"But you didn't say it before," I whisper.

"Because you shocked the hell out of me. I mean come on, Gucci, look at you. You're the definition of beauty personified and then look at me... I'm nothing."

"I am looking at you, Vincent, and if you can't see what I see, then something is wrong with you."

"A girl like you shouldn't love a guy like me, Gucci. You're fine wine, silk and perfection. I'm me. I live in the jungle and have a small hut. I don't have a mansion and flashy cars. I'm a simple guy—" I silence him by kissing him, pouring all the love I feel for him into this kiss. He needs to know I don't care about any of that stuff, all I want is *him*.

Chapter Nineteen

Vincent

By the time we land at least four hostesses glare at us as we exit the plane. Yeah, they all knew we were fucking the whole way. I wrap my arm around my girl and pull her into my side as we walk to baggage claim. It feels fucking amazing to know she loves me and doesn't give a fuck about what I drive or where I live. I never thought the day would come where a woman would capture my attention and have no judgment toward my lifestyle choices.

There are cameras everywhere through here and I know it is merely a matter of time before her brother is alerted. I have no doubt he will be tracking us through the live video feed, I'm actually counting on it. I have a plan in place and it ensures that I'm not ambushed by her family. I may love her, but I won't take any unmercenary risks where her safety is concerned. My Gucci is a spit fire and if a gun is pointed at me, I have no fucking doubt she would stand in the line of fire and take the shot for me. If that were to happen, no one would survive my fucking wrath.

"Are you sure this plan is going to work?" The hesitation in her voice is clear, she loves me but she is still loyal to her family and I can respect that.

"It will work, give it two days tops and they will find us. Bishop thinks you are flying in on Saturday, we have two days to set up and be ready for when they come." I'm fucking certain of that. I know Bishop has been trying to track us and find any way he can to bring her home. Excitement thrums through me knowing in a matter of a couple days I will finally come face to face with the fucker that had a hand in selling my sister. No one here in the US, aside from Marco, knows I'm alive. I'm sure when her family runs my face through facial recognition software they are going to lose their fucking minds and I can't wait for the fallout.

⸻

Two Days....

Exactly like I knew they would, they came for her.

The motion sensor alarms blare throughout the cabin I own in Cazenovia. I haven't slept a wink knowing they were coming. I have everything in place and ready. I silence the alarms and head into the bedroom to wake Carlina only to find her standing at the end of the bed dressed in a pair of jeans and a white knit sweater. Her eyes are wide and full of fear. I close the distance between us and wrap my arms around her. She holds me tight and buries her face in my chest. We have about three minutes before they get here. I wish I had the time to hold her and soothe away her worries, but I don't. I push her back and cup her face before I claim her lips in a kiss of ownership that only lasts a few seconds. I pull back and bend down so we are eye level.

"I swear on my sister I won't let them take you from me." Tears fall from her eyes as she grips my forearms.

"Promise me you won't die. I need to know that you and I will walk out of this together, Vincent. I... can't lose you." I smash my lips to hers again and quickly pull back when the alarm goes again, alerting me to the fact they are a minute out.

"I promise, now I have to go. Wait here until I call for you." I don't wait for a reply as I rush from the room, turn off the alarm system and head outside to wait. I check my watch and smirk, fuckers think because it's four in the morning I would be asleep. I have a Glock strapped to each hip, knives are strapped everywhere on my body. I have a backup gun strapped to my ankle and my rifle in my hand, ready. I stand front and center at the top of the stairs. I know they have sent others through the dirt road around the back, no point in hiding in the shadows, plus I have this whole fucking place rigged and can take them out at any given moment. I stand tall and hold my head high when I hear them approaching. I want to laugh because they think leaving their cars on the road is going to give them the element of surprise.

They are fucking rookies. If they knew a fucking thing about me, they would know trying to attack me at my own home is their worst mistake. Every property I own is set up with a fail-safe to make sure I always have a way out in case of an ambush. I promised my girl I wouldn't kill her brothers but I never promised I wouldn't hurt them or kill their men. The closer they get the more my mind clears, this is second nature to me now. Nothing distracts me from a kill. I love the numbness the jobs bring, it's the only time my mind is clear and I'm not plotting my next move on how to take my father down. I'm fucking good at what I do but even I am only one man and don't have the numbers to go after him on my own.

I spot the first lot of guys breaking through the left side of the trees, I can feel their guns pointed at me. I'm wrapped up in Kevlar from my chest to my toes, their only guaranteed kill shot is to the head. The baseball cap I'm currently wearing is made of Kevlar as well, so they better not miss. The second line comes from the right. I don't move from my position, I hold firm and wait. I know they will come from the front. There is no way Bishop would stay home and risk looking like a bitch. I'm fucking banking on him and the rest of her brothers to be here. Sure enough, the final line breaks through the dense trees that surround the cabin. I want to fucking snort when I see the prick in the middle of them all in a three-piece fucking suit!

Bishop is bigger in person then I thought he would be. His hair is slicked back flat against his head. The only lighting out here is from the moon, all the lights inside are off so I can't get a good read on his face. To his right holding an AK that is pointed right at my head is the underboss, King. He looks nothing like the others but I got to give it to him, he's just as big as his older brother. I turn to Bishop's left and spot one of the twins, Knight. It may be dark out but even I can tell this guy thrives in the darkness just from how he holds himself. The one that has me worried is the one that doesn't carry the same last name but shares blood with them. He stands beside Knight, his gaze fixed on me with a cocky smirk. Gage... he isn't tanned like the others and doesn't carry the same air of arrogance around him. My attention is pulled from him as the two guys beside King move forward, I recognize them from the photos I have and videos. Luka and Mav. Luka actually seems like a loyal guy and cares for this family but Mav, he is a fucking snake and needs to be put down.

"You hand her over now and I'll make it quick. Try to fuck with me and I'll draw it out until you're begging for death." I cut my gaze back to Bishop and smile, the *don't fuck with me* tone may work on others but not me. He moves closer still keeping a good distance between us, his upper lip is pulled back in snarl.

"I'll give you five minutes to convince me not to kill you and all your bitches, how about that?" Like music to my ears, every gun around me cocks readying to lay led into my body if their Don should command it.

"Where the fuck is my sister?" The anger in the Don's tone sends a thrill through me. I ignore everything else as I step off the porch. I feel them all move closer as I move toward Bishop. I stop when there is three feet between us. Up close I can see him clearly. His eyes are almost pitch black, tattoos peek out of the collar of his shirt. He may be able to fool others but I know beneath that suit jacket he's packing and definitely has a gun stashed in his waistband. Bishop and I stand eye level, he's trying to figure out what angle I'm playing here.

"Exactly where she wants to be." I make sure he can hear the cockiness in my voice. The sound of a scream from inside the cabin has my blood turning to ice. I take off, not caring that my back is to my enemy. I feel Bishop behind me as I leap up the steps and smash the door open, the light in the room is on so I beeline for there, my mind blanks and I don't even think when I see the sight of this cunt on top of my girl.

Chapter Twenty

Carlina

I struggle beneath him trying to get him off me, but he's too big and caught me by surprise. Everything Vin has taught over the months has gone out the window, my fear overrides my rational thought. I cry out when his grip on my wrist turns punishing, a gunshot sounds out then blood is splattering across my face as the guy pinning me to the bed goes limp, a second later he's thrown off me and Vincent is there pulling me to him. I bury my face in his chest and cling to him sobbing as his hold on me tightens. I can feel the anger wafting off him.

"You're okay, Gucci. I got you." Hearing his softly spoken words only causes me to sob more, I have no idea who the hell that guy was. "Are you hurt?" I nod against his chest, he pushes me back and grips the tops of my shoulders and bends so we are eye level. Movement in the corner of my eye catches my attention and I gasp, I break away from Vin and run to Bishop. I launch myself at him when I'm close enough. He catches me and holds me tightly, we stay like this for a few minutes until I'm pulled from his hold and King is there hugging me. I break away from King and shoot him a wink as I go for Knight. He stands in front of me, stiff and riddled with tension. I see it in his eyes—guilt. I reach out and grip both of his hands in mine ignoring the ache in my wrist, he won't meet my gaze and it pisses me off.

"Knight, look at me." Seconds pass before he finally does as I ask, the torment in his gaze spears me right in the chest. "We'll find him." My words seem to spark some life back into his dark eyes. He drops my hands, then hugs me tight. Knight is the brother who doesn't do touching or hugs so the fact he is the one who initiated this shocks me. He and I break apart and I turn to the last, Gage. He stands there looking unsure on what to do. I make the choice for him when I hug him. He doesn't move for a moment clearly shocked but it only takes a second before his arms are wrapping around me and then tension in his body slowly drains away. I pull back from him and take a couple steps backward. My four brothers stand there with murderous looks in their eyes. I peer over my shoulder and that's when I remember Vin is behind me.

"Take Carlina outside," Bishop orders. Gage takes a step forward as I take one back. I pin him with a warning look and being the smart guy that he is he stops moving and looks to Bishop. "Don't fuck around, Carlina, go now."

"You don't tell her what the fuck to do!" Vin growls.

King and Knight act fast, they draw their guns and point them at Vin. I rush to block him. He swerves around me and pushes me behind him. "You fucking prick, you pull a gun while she is right in the middle!"

"I'm a dead shot, I'd never have hit her." The sureness in King's tone has Vin vibrating with rage. I try to move out from behind him but Vin snaps his arms backward and holds me flush against him, not allowing me to move.

"Stay the fuck there, Gucci," Vin snaps.

"Kill the fucker!" Bishop orders, my blood turns to ice, everything inside me is screaming for me to do something but my body won't respond as fear takes hold of me. I hear movement and then curses before Gage speaks.

"Put the fucking guns down, now!" I could fucking hug the shit out of Gage right now.

"You want a bullet as well? Kiara isn't here to save you this time, Gage. You have two fucking seconds or I put you both down." The tone of Bishop's voice tells me he isn't my loving brother anymore, he's in Don mode.

"Pull the fucking trigger and she will hate you forever. Take him back with us, *alive* and put him in the bunker." *No!* I use all my weight and pull backward until Vin's grip on me drops. I dart around him and stand beside Gage.

"Gucci—" I eye Bishop, Knight and King as I cut Vin off.

"You take him to the bunker, then you better be ready to strap me to the chair next to him, put a bullet in his head and you can put one in mine!" The three of them stand there with their perfect poker faces, the only sign that they are shocked by my declaration is the sudden twitch of King's upper lip. Knight blinks rapidly for a second and Bishop's hand twitches on the trigger of his gun.

"You have no fucking idea who he is—"

"I know exactly who he is, Bishop. He's told me everything," I defend.

"Did he tell you he was coming after me, after our fucking family?" I nibble on my bottom lip nervously as I nod. Bishop grunts in anger before he steps forward. At the same moment he moves to me, I feel Vin at my back. Bishop pauses and eyes Vin over my head. "This can go two ways. I put a bullet in your fucking head now or you agree to be interrogated." I open my mouth to protest but he shoots me a glare and continues. "Those are his choices, Carlina. You will obey whatever the fuck I say. He is the enemy here—"

"But you can let a fucking Russian live in our house?" At my outburst Knight steps forward and pins me with a look of warning.

"She isn't what you think," he grits out.

"I know exactly who Katarina Antonov is. I know more than all of you fucking think because of *him*." My three brothers cut their gazes to Vin eyeing him with nothing but hatred in their gazes. "I also know that you need an in with the Russians. Help us and we'll help you get Gage inside the Bratva." All four of them are staring at me like I'm some foreign invader. I spin around giving them my back as I peer up at Vin. His gaze is sharp and I can tell from the hard set of his jaw he doesn't like this situation one bit. I can see it in his eyes he is pissed off at what I just told my brothers. "I had no choice," I say quietly.

"There is always a choice, Gucci. You just made yours by selling me out to your brothers." I flinch at his cold tone, I didn't see another way out of this. Vin has connections that can help my family but my family can also help Vin. Problem is, Bishop and Vin are so pig headed they can't put their pride and ego aside and admit they need each other's help.

Chapter Twenty-One

Vincent

I want to strangle the fuck out of her right now!

Her big doe eyes implore me to see that she only did this to help me. I know she meant well but all she has done is cause more problems. Bishop will never let it rest now. We may have had a shot at walking away from this, but now, he will do whatever it takes to get the information out of me by using his sister against me.

"Vincent, please—" I shake my head cutting her off. This is a conversation we need to have in private not in front of her brother's.

"It's done." My moment of distraction cost me, a shot rings out and I'm stumbling back a step as Gage swoops in wrapping his arms around my girls waist and dragging her from the room. My shoulder burns from the gun shot, I cut my gaze to Bishop and grit my teeth, the fucker is smiling wide with his gun still pointed at me.

"Let me go!" Carlina struggles in Gage's hold, he's trying his fucking best to hold her tight without hurting her. I step forward ready to lay the fucker out but King cuts me off with the barrel of his gun pressed against my forehead. I keep my gaze on my girl, she goes pale and limp in Gage's hold with tears streaming down her cheeks as she looks to me.

"Bishop, please! I'll be good. I'll never run away again, please don't hurt him." He won't kill me... yet, he needs the information I have before he'll deliver the final blow. The only reason I'm not fighting back right now and shooting each of them to get to my girl is because I can't risk her getting hurt in the crossfire.

"Go now, Carlina, we'll talk about this later." His tone is firm and final but she doesn't listen, Bishop never takes his eyes off me.

"Bish, please. I'll never speak to him again, just let him go!" she screams. Bishop finally pulls his gaze from me to shoot Gage a look, he nods and drags my girl from the room. I push forward but King shoves the gun harder against my head earning himself a fucking death glare from me.

"You fucking touch her——"

"You won't fucking do shit!" Knight cuts in as soon as Carlina is out of the room. King turns to Bishop for his next order. I use that moment to strike out, ignoring the burn in my shoulder as I disarm King and turn the gun on him. Bishop and Knight both have their guns on me as I push the barrel of the gun into King's head like he did mine.

"Like I said, you fucking touch her and I will kill you," I snarl. King's eyes burn with unfiltered rage. He's fucking furious I disarmed him even with a shot to the shoulder. I learnt long ago to dissociate myself from pain. "Now, here is how this is going to play out." Before I can finish, Bishop speaks, his eyes are so dark they are almost black with hatred.

"You pull that fucking trigger and I promise you I won't kill you for years. I'll make you my new play thing and even get my sister to watch as I fucking break you apart piece by piece."

"You can try," I grit out.

"You're out manned," Knight says.

"Do you really think you got in here because you're that good?" I laugh but there is no humor to it, I don't give them a chance to answer. "I let you in here, the only reason you all are still breathing is because of *her*." King and Knight both look confused. Bishop on the other hand looks smug and that is slightly unsettling.

"Rookie error. You kidnapped her and were meant to use her against me but you didn't." He scoffs and shakes his head whilst I stand here gritting my teeth. "You fell in love with my fucking sister." The disgust in his tone is clear. "Now, let me tell *you* how this is going to play out." The smug fuck smirks as he uses my own words against me. "You are either going to come willingly or I bring my sister back in here and... persuade you with other means." I reel my arm back and smack the butt of the gun against King's head, he drops to his knees in front of me as blood gushes from his forehead. I never take my eyes off Bishop as I move the gun from King to Bishop.

"Call her back in here now!" He's not even fazed that I have his brother on his knees and at my mercy with a gun trained on him. I make sure to keep an eye on Knight, that fucker is a wild card.

"Not gonna happen, the whole place is surrounded even if you take us out, you'll never make it out of here and I promise you you'll never find my sister."

"Where the fuck is she, Bishop?" I snap.

"Safe." His one-word response has me seeing red, I ready myself to squeeze the trigger and end the son of bitch but then Gage walks in. He pauses at the scene in front of him, rolls his eyes and moves so he is in the middle of all three guns. He looks to his brothers and shakes his head before focusing on me.

"Put the gun down, there will be no bunker—"

"Like fuck!" Bishop snaps but Gage ignores him and pushes on.

"No one will shoot you... again if you can answer this one question." I eye him warily for a moment. The fact Bishop hasn't pulled rank yet leads me to believe he is just as curious to see what Gage says.

"What is it?"

"What are you willing to do if it means you get to be with her?" Well, that wasn't what I expected him to say. I don't even hesitate to answer.

"Whatever it takes. I don't need your permission or even want it, she's mine." I make sure to meet Bishop's gaze as I say the last part. I don't stop him when King slowly climbs to his feet, his upper lip is pulled back in a snarl and his eyes are narrowed.

"You may not want it or need it, but it would make her life easier. She may love you but she won't turn her back on family either."

"He is not coming back with us!" Knight declares. Gage turns his back to me to face Bishop. Either he is stupid as fuck or has balls of steel to turn his back to me when I could shoot the dick in the head without pause.

"If you kill him, Carlina will run, you have to know that. If you don't want him at the house then bring him back to the gym, he can stay there." I'm fucking speechless at the fact Gage is standing here defending me. I don't fucking trust any of them and he is a wild card. I wasn't able to find out much about him like the others. He doesn't even have a fucking record, not even a speeding fucking ticket.

"She won't be running anywhere. She is home and now the war begins. You bring him out, breathing or not, I don't give a fuck." Bishop is full of shit and everyone knows it. He needs me alive to figure out how the fuck I know about all their secrets. Bishop and King leave the room, Knight lingers for a moment and I can see it in his eyes that he is dying to ask me something.

"Just say whatever it is and then go," Gage prompts his brother. Knight shoots him a scathing look but asks none the less.

"Can you find my brother?" No matter how hard he tried, he can't disguise the hope in his voice.

"I don't know," I answer honestly. He nods before leaving and then it's just me and Gage. He turns to face me, we stand here sizing each other up.

"If what they say about you is true, then I need your help."

"What exactly do *they* say?" I hedge.

"That the *Bloodhound* can find anyone. You're the one who they send in when everything else fails." I push my lips to the side and nod, not agreeing or denying his claim. "Let's go get that wound tended to before Bishop really does kill you." I snort and he shakes his head. "You are playing a dangerous game fucking with him and King, they won't let you near her."

"They can try and fucking stop me, but Carlina is mine."

"Yeah, I can't wait to watch this shit go down," he says as he walks out leaving me standing in my room alone. The sounds of shouting outside draws my attention. I move toward the window, pull the blind back and peek out before cursing and racing outside. I pause next to Gage at the top of the steps. My girl has Luka on his knees with a gun pointed to the back of his head. Bishop, Knight and King stand in front of her. I tilt my head slightly to get a better look and that's when I see she has a gun in her other hand pointed at her brothers. "You need to handle that," Gage says quietly I nod.

"Where the hell is he?" she shouts sounding hysteric.

"He's alive," King snaps. Deciding to put an end to this shit, I move the down the steps and bite my tongue to keep my pained hiss from spilling free thanks to jolting my fucking shoulder. She doesn't see me until I push my way between Knight and Bishop ignoring their mumbles of me being a dick. The tension flees her body at the sight of me. I grab the gun she has pointed at her brothers and shove it in my waistband, she drops the other one she has pointed at Luka's head to launch herself at me. I stumble back a step but don't drop her, I manage to hold her up around her waist with my one arm. She whacks my hat off my head before she smashes her lips to mine, I smile against her mouth when I hear her brother's cursing behind us.

Chapter Twenty-Two

Carlina

Vin places me back on my feet, but I cling to his shirt not wanting to let go of him. I dart my gaze to his shoulder and anger surges inside me.

"Bishop is such an asshole!" I growl.

"I can hear you, Carlina," Bishop snaps. I wink up at Vin, earning a light laugh. I interlock my fingers through his and turn to face my brothers. Luka stands there glaring at me. I shoot him an apologetic smile and shrug my shoulders. I turn to Bishop but his gaze is focused solely on Vin. I need to fix this before more shit goes wrong. I open my mouth but clamp it closed when Vin speaks.

"I'll help you take Vinny and Pauly out if you return my

sister." Bishop's face pulls taught, I can see from the look in his eyes he has no idea what Vin is talking about.

"Why the fuck would I have your sister? Vinny Murelo doesn't have a daughter and up until a few days ago we all thought his son was dead. Clearly we were misled about that." The accusation in Bish's voice is clear. Vin's grip on my hand tightens to almost punishing, but I grit my teeth and push through it as I know this situation is fucking hard for him.

"Your family... *bought* her." Disgust drips from Vin's tone. Bishop takes two steps forward with his shoulders stiff, jaw locked tight and anger brewing his eyes.

"I don't fucking deal in the skin trade. I don't have your sister but you have *mine*." Vin doesn't falter.

"Then give me the records of your father's transactions. Help me and I'll help you." Bish eyes Vin for a second before he answers.

"I'll help you find your sister on one condition."

"No," Vin grits out, a dark smile crests across Bishop's face. I look to King and Knight and they both seem as confused as I am.

"Then I won't help you and you still die." I gasp.

"Bishop no——" I snap my mouth closed when Bishop pins me with a warning look.

"He had a chance, he refused."

"Refused what?" I shout, Vin answers me instead of Bishop.

"He'll help me find my sister if I leave *his* sister and not come back for you." My eyes widen in shock. Bishop doesn't even look ashamed, if anything he looks smug as fuck. I pull my phone from my pocket and scroll my contact list. I feel all their eyes on me as I hit dial and bring it to my ear, as I wait for them to answer I shout out to Gage.

"Can you give us a ride to the gym?"

"Like fuck—" I hold a finger up to Bishop when she answers the phone, silencing him.

"Hello?" Bishop's eyes are narrowed.

"Hey, Kiara." Bish's eyes widen slightly and his mouth is ajar in shock that I would stoop as low as to call his fiancée, my best friend.

"Car, what's going on? Are you okay?" My heart melts at her concern.

"I would be better if Bishop didn't just shoot my boyfriend and try to get him to leave me. Oh and he wants to put him in the bunker and kill him." Bishop stands before me grinding his teeth, rage is brewing in his dark gaze and it brings a smile to my face.

"Where is he?" she growls. I smile as I drop Vin's hand and walk to my brother. I hold the phone out to him with a bright smile.

"Kiara would like to speak to you." He glares down at me as he snatches the phone from me and storms off.

I'm huddled into Vin's side waiting for Bishop come back and I'll admit I'm feeling slightly smug about my trump card. Calling Kiara was the last move I had and I think it paid off. I can tell from how stiff Vin is that his shoulder is causing him some severe discomfort. I'm about to ask him if he wants me to take a look at it when Bishop comes back. His face is a mask of rage and annoyance, I fight to keep the triumphant expression off my face. He stops next to the others and whispers something in King's ear. As per usual, I can't decipher King's expression, the guy has a poker face like no other. He gives Bishop a curt nod before walking away to where their men are huddled at the side of the cabin. Worry gnaws at me when Bish goes to Knight and says something I can't hear and Knight smiles wickedly before Gage darts his gaze to me when Bishop approaches him next. Gage's eyes harden as he stands there and listen's to what B is saying before reluctantly nodding.

"Carlina, a word?" I tense in Vin's hold. He gives me a reassuring squeeze before I pull away and move toward Bishop. He holds my phone out to me and some of the worry begins to fade when I think all he wants is to return my phone and curse me out about calling Kiara. I reach out to grab my phone, Bishop moves quicker than I can blink. He drops the phone, snags my wrist, spins me around and holds me against him with my back to his chest. I struggle to get free, Vin storms toward us but stops when Knight, King and the other guys surround him with all their guns drawn.

"Bishop, no!" I scream. "If you do this, I will hate you forever. I swear to god I will run and you will never find me again!" I sob as tears cascade down my cheeks. Vin's gaze is locked onto mine as he stands in the man-made circle with guns trained on him. I know if I shout for him to help me, he will try to fight his way to me even if it cost him his life.

"Look how well that worked out for you the first time, Car. You run and come home with *our* enemy's son. You did good, sister, you brought me leverage and now, all we need to do is use your little boy toy to get what we want." I search Vin's gaze a moment trying to read what he is think-ing, I try to convey to him with my own eyes that I will do everything I can to set him free. My brother is a bastard for doing this. He got his girl and now he doesn't care who he has to hurt in order to control his own fucking kingdom.

"Let him go. I'll give you all the information I have. You don't need him Bishop..." I take a deep breath and mouth

I'm sorry to Vin as I speak the next part loud enough for everyone to hear. "Vincent is a nobody. His father never wanted him and didn't care he faked his own death. If you're doing this because you think I love him, I don't." An ache so deep and raw explodes in my chest as the lie slips so easily from my mouth. "I did what I had to do in order to stay alive. He wanted to use me to get to you. I turned the tables... I tempted him and he fell for it."

Vincent's expression remains neutral but his eyes, they burn with... agony. My words have caused him more pain than the bullet he took for me. He has to know that I am only saying this to try and save him from the wrath of my brothers. I love Vin and I want a life with him, but I will sacrifice my own happiness if it means he gets to live and go free.

"See, I would have brought that bullshit about thirty minutes ago except." I stiffen in Bishop's hold and I know he felt the shift in me. He whispers the last part for only me to hear. "Your eyes betray you sister, I can see it in the way you subtly shift toward him. You watch his every move and when you couldn't see him your eyes automatically sought him out. Thing is, he does the same to you except he is willing to die to save you. I'm going to use his love for you to crush him and win this fucking war." My heart shatters inside my chest.

I watch as the guy's wrestle Vin to the ground. He fights with everything he has to remain standing but there's too many of them. Tears trek silently down my cheeks as I watch the man I have fallen so deeply in love with be beaten and treated like a dog, all because of me. Vincent is only here because I asked him to come with me to help find Rook. I did this to us.

I ruined us.

Chapter Twenty-Three

Carlina

Four weeks....

Every day starts the same, I wake to pounding on my bedroom door and refuse to even acknowledge it. I don't want to see any of them, none of them understand what being back in this godforsaken house is like for me. Being in this room sucks the fucking life out of me. Dark and horrible nightmares assault me every night. I don't sleep—I can't. Every time I close my eyes all I see is him and how he destroyed me, tore my innocence from me and made me do despicable things. I've never slept without nightmares until... Vin. The thought of him has me fighting back tears and forcing the lump down in my throat. Watching as King and Knight dragged his battered and broken, unconscious body to a waiting car that night they came for me, broke me worse than Tony ever did.

I fought with everything I had and even managed to land a few hits on Bishop and broke free. I made it five steps before Gage was there hauling me against his chest. I fought against him—bit him, punched, slapped and clawed at his skin until the fight left my body and I sagged against him. He held me while I sobbed for my man. I passed out from exhaustion as Gage carried me away from the vehicle that held my whole heart in it.

"Car, can you please... talk to me?" I roll over and hold the pillow over my head to block out Kiara. I know I shouldn't be mad at her but I am. No one in this fucking house has told me where Vin is or if he's even alive. I tried for the first four days to beg, plead and downright fight for answers but no one would tell me a thing! The only fucking person who seemed to feel a small amount of guilt was Knight's girl, Koby. Allison just grabs her daughter and scurries the other way when she sees me, I don't blame her though. I wouldn't want my child watching a mad woman lose her shit either.

After the sixth day here, I locked myself in my room and refused to leave it. King, Knight and Gage have all tried to coax me out but I ignore them. Kiara tries daily to get me to talk to her but I can't. That first day I begged her to help me, to try find out from Bishop where he was keeping Vin but she said she couldn't and that put a wedge between us. I know she has always loved my brother since we were kids but... a small part of me thought our friendship meant more to her.

The sun is beginning to set and I still haven't gotten out of bed, what's the point?

I don't want to fucking exist if he isn't breathing, before Vincent I had nothing, I had my brothers but that wasn't enough. I was a ghost, no one ever saw me for *me*. I was a dirty secret that needed to be hidden. But then Vin came along, and he saw *me*, not the mafia heiress. He saw the real me. He showed me the world and didn't give a fuck about my last name or where I came from. The man lit a fire inside me that burned so bright and hot, I never in a million years thought my brother would be the one to extinguish the fire inside me and destroy the happiness I finally found. I finally found a man who loved me, adored me and gave me all of him, only for Bishop to rip him away. Tears leak from the corners of my eyes, my chest aches so badly that I can hardly breathe.

"Where are you, baby?" I whisper into the empty room that holds nothing but nightmares for me. A knock sounds at the door but I ignore it. I know it's Martha bringing me my dinner but I barely eat or drink. I eat a small amount each day only because King said if I didn't, he would send Bishop up to hold me down while they force fed me. Another knock sounds out but I ignore it. Martha will go away if I keep quiet. I snap my tear-filled gaze to the door when I hear the lock click, my breath hitches as I watch the thing slowly open. A stupid part of me hopes and prays it's Vin because he escaped my brothers and is coming for me. Hope flees my body when they walk in. I turn to face the window and watch as the sun finally disappears.

"I said I couldn't help you because at that time I couldn't." I keep my back to Kiara and the other two not wanting to hear what they have to say. I hear their footsteps pad toward me but I keep my gaze focused out the window.

Kiara sits down next to me on the bed. I eye the other two out of the corner of my eye. Allison looks pissed, I didn't think the girl had it in her to angry. Koby leans against the wall with her arms crossed over chest, her baby bump visible through the tight black tee she wears. "I had to bide my time and wait, Car. He would have known what I was up to. Look at me!" I slowly turn away from the window to face my so-called best friend, her eyes are filled with sorrow when she finally gazes upon me. She clasps both my hands in hers and squeezes them. "I need you to get in the shower and change as fast as you can." I scoff as I tear my hands free and face the window again.

"Fuck it, let her reek of shit when she sees her man again, I don't give a fuck." I snap my gaze to Koby only to find her vibrant green eyes already on me with a brow raised. "You want someone to coddle you and hold your hand, then look to Ally and Kiara because I don't do that shit." I snort, she is fucking perfect for Knight. "Get your ass up and shower because we have a small amount of time before the guys get back and realize Gage was full of shit." I furrow my brow in confusion, Koby rolls her eyes and pins Kiara with a look. Kiara chuckles, stands and offers me her hand. I stare at before meeting her eyes waiting for an explanation.

"We know where your man is, shower and change and we'll take you to him but you need to hurry, Carlina!" I'm on my feet in an instant and barging past the three of them. I strip off my disgusting sleepwear I have been wearing for days as I go. I hear them laugh behind me but I don't give a fuck. I'm getting my man back and that's all that matters.

After showering and changing at lightning speed the four of us race from the house and jump into Allison's Range Rover. It feels weird to be clean, in fresh clothes and I even brushed my teeth. My hair is a wet unbrushed mess that is piled on top of my hair but I don't give a shit, for the first time in weeks I feel something other than grief and pain.

"Where are we going?" Allison and Kiara gasp at the sound of my voice. Koby, who is sitting beside me in the back seat shoots me a wink. I like her already. She doesn't bullshit or mince words, I like that.

"We're going to get your man and clearly piss off three of your brothers." I smirk a little, Allison is a badass. I didn't think the girl had it in her but it's good to see she can hold her own. She will need to because King is a pushy bastard.

"How did you find him?" I ask softly. Kiara leans around her seat so she can see me in the back, her eyes are filled with remorse.

"Bishop wouldn't tell me anything when you first got back. He kept tight lipped about the whole thing. Ally tried to get information from King but he wouldn't budge. Koby even tried to beat it out of Knight." I turn to Koby with a smile on my face, she just shrugs her shoulders like it's no big deal that she tried to kick my brother's ass.

"He's lucky I'm pregnant. If I wasn't we both know I would have had him on his ass," Koby snaps.

"Riiight," Kiara and Ally say unison, earning a glare from Koby.

"So, how did you find out?" I prompt.

"Gage." I cock my head to the side confused as to why she said his name. Kiara smiles sadly. "I know the guys don't know him well, but I do. Ally and Koby are close with Gage as well. We didn't even have to ask him to help us, Car. He got the shit beaten out of him for defying Bishop and not helping them put your man down." I reel back in shock.

"What?"

"Gage said he could never hurt you like that and Bishop made him pay for defying his orders." I can feel the anger radiating off of her. "Gage found the location where Vin is being held. He sent me the coordinates and created a diversion so he could distract Bish and the others while we go rescue your man." A feeling of guilt washes over me. I haven't exactly treated him like shit but I haven't tried to get to know him or even make him feel welcome and yet, Gage is here trying to help me and paid for not getting involved. I vow to myself right here that I will do better, I will try to get to know my older brother and make him feel like one of us.

Chapter Twenty-Four

Vincent

"It won't work, you need to set the ambush and wait while they tuck tail and run!" I grit out. Bishop narrows his eyes at me. I glare right back at the asshole. He has no idea how to ambush and there is no fucking way I am going out there and risking my life for his dumb ass.

"What the fuck do you suggest then?" King pipes up beside his brother. I keep my gaze on the Don as I answer the underboss.

"Simple, you draw them both out with the promise of agreeing to a deal. You tell them that you want in on the skin trade. Once they are out in the open it will be as easy as picking them off one by fucking one." King turns to side eye Bishop, but he ignores his brother keeping his focus on me.

"You get Pauly and Vinny to the meet and you keep up your end, you have my word I'll give you what you want." I grind my teeth and clench my fists at my sides to keep my anger in check, I didn't go through all of this to lose the one thing I want most.

"She was never yours to begin with," I grit out as I turn and head back toward the back of the warehouse where Knight sits with Luka. Both of them scour the web daily for any picture, video or any kind of evidence from the local police departments that may mention Rook. I've put through a fake job application through to the agency that employs me, I'm offering a fifteen million for the head of Rook Murdoch. I've had at least hundred people claim the job but none of them have been able to find Rook. I know how they feel losing a sibling and not knowing where they are or if they are even alive. That feeling consumes you daily and eats away at your soul every fucking second of every day.

"Any bites on the job?" Knight tries to hide his hope but the small spark in his eyes shows me he still has hope for his twin being alive. In all honestly, he could have been thrown into the ocean that night and dragged out to sea by the current. That is the most likely outcome but I won't be the one to crush his hope because I've never lost hope that one day I will find Selena.

"Nah, man, not yet." His eyes darken, he gives me a curt nod and goes back to work. I look to my left where I spot Bishop's right hand man Mav. Something about him seems so fucking familiar and I just can't fucking place where I know the guy from.

"They're here!" I spin toward where Bishop and King

stand around the table with blueprints spread out and their men standing with them to find Gage at the head of the table. His face is contorted with unease and worry, Bishop gets right in his face.

"Who?" he snarls, Gage cuts a quick glance to me before looking back to Bishop.

"The girls." Bishop reels back, anger is evident in his features. Gage stands tall ready and waiting for Bishop to lose his shit.

"I fucking knew you would go running to them." Gage doesn't even look put out that he got caught. He tried to get Bishop and the others to go out and check out a bullshit sighting of Vinny. All I had to do was call Marco and check where Vinny was and that put an end to Gage's plan. He came clean straight away. He and Bishop traded a few punches before we pulled them apart. "If this plan falls apart because of you, I'll make you dig your own grave before I bury you in it." I don't get the tension between these two. King and Knight seem to be fine with Gage but Bishop holds a lot of resentment toward his half-brother.

"You know what, after everything I am about to do for this fucking family the least you could do is put your shit with me aside. I had no fucking idea who she was to you!" Gage yells.

"I told you to watch out for her, not fuck her!" Bishop roars as he gets right in Gage's face. They both stand there, forehead to forehead vibrating with rage. I move forward to break them up but King places a hand on my shoulder shaking his head.

"They need to sort this shit now before he goes. Bishop needs to do this and Gage needs to hear it." King speaks quietly so only I can hear him. I give a curt nod and watch the two brothers.

"She fucking needed me, you don't get it. You weren't fucking there, Bishop! She was broken and fucked up. You should have gone to her and not been a pussy hiding in the shadows watching from afar while I brought her back. I fucking brought her back from the hole she put herself in. Me, not you." I can hear the anguish in Gage's voice and that's when it clicks. Gage slept with his brother's fiancée.

"She wasn't supposed to be brought into this. I wanted her to have a life before I came for her and you fucked it up."

"Nah, B, you fucked up because she wanted *you*!" Bishop moves back a step, clearly this is new information to the big fucker. "She cried out for you in her sleep for months, she begged for you to come save her. One night when it was too much, I tried to comfort her and shit went down. It was never me she wanted, she was picturing you, Bishop. I knew that from the start but I couldn't stop. Kiara has been in love with you since she was eight years old. It always has been and always will be you, Bishop. I will never be more to her than a brother or a best friend and I get that now." Bishop stands there stiff and tense with his hands balled into fists at his side, that has got to be a bitter pill to swallow knowing your brother slept with your girl.

"You want my forgiveness, you do your fucking job and end this shit. You betrayed me, Gage. The only reason you are still breathing now is because of *her*. Don't fucking mistake my kindness toward my girl for weakness because I will murder you and make it look like an accident so she will never know it was me. Bring me home his head and I'll forgive you, fail me and you won't like the consequences."

"Incoming!" Luka shouts as he watches the video surveillance. There are cameras set up all around the warehouse and it's fitted with an alarm system that I set up myself. I even upgraded the one at Bishop's house and taught Knight and Luka how to run the system. I was shocked to learn that Koby is the best hacker. Luka didn't like admitting that but the Russian girl knows her shit and is really fucking good. I was even more fucking shocked to learn that King's girl helps him extract information. The girl looks a fucking teacher and yet she gets down and dirty torturing people.

"Everyone, get in position now!" Bishop's voice booms around the warehouse. Men scatter their positions while King and I stay in the middle, where we are. A moment later, Knight, Gage and Bishop join us. I roll my eyes as Bishop adjusts his suit jacket, how he can be comfortable in that fucking monkey suit I'll never know. Knight rubs his hands together in a gleeful gesture and rolls his neck side to side.

"Oh my girl is so getting fucked for this." King shakes his head and laughs at his brother's antics.

"Allison is so not coming for a month." Knight and Gage both laugh at King's declaration.

"Kiara is going to fucking pay for this stunt. the little minx thinks she can break into my office and steal my keys, she has another thing coming." Gage snorts and whispers,

"She stole your balls years ago." Bishop cuts him a glare over his shoulder before the lights are turned off and we all stand here shrouded in darkness. My pulse kicks up and my body begins to thrum with awareness knowing my girl is right outside. It's been a month since I have been able to touch her, kiss her or smell her scent and it has been fucking agony not being able to see her. I watch the video feed of their house daily and she hasn't stepped foot out of her room for three weeks until tonight. She looked so fucking bad ass, tight black jeans, a white crop top and black leather boots. My cock is getting hard from just thinking about her. I just hope she doesn't use the gun I saw shoved into her waistband as they left the house on me.

At the sound of footfalls outside the warehouse, Gage and King grow still beside me. I can feel Bishop and Knight in front of me but I can't see them, there are no windows in here so the moon can't even grant some reprieve from the dark. We hear a key being shoved into the lock, then the door creaks loudly as it's pulled open. We all remain silent as we listen to the girls' hushed whispers.

"I am going to kill my brothers for this stunt." I roll my lips over my teeth to keep the smile from breaking free at the sound of my girl's voice.

"Find a light switch," another girl whispers, then we hear them shuffling around. They wouldn't last five minutes in the field, they would have been caught as soon as the sound of their footsteps were heard.

"You all sound like a fucking pack of elephants, stop moving!" I don't know who it is that spoke, but I can feel Knight shaking with silent laughter in front of me, so I guess it's his girl.

"Why?" King stiffens beside me, the voice must belong to his girl.

"Because you pack of idiots, this is a set up!" Knights girl hisses.

"How do you know?" I'm assuming this voice belongs to Bishop's girl, Kiara.

"Because there is no way they would have left a prisoner here without a guard inside and outside, there is no sign of life and I don't smell shit. I can tell you now, Knight wouldn't be washing some guys junk unless the both of you think King and Bishop would?" Now I begin to shake with silent laughter, Knight's girl is fucking perceptive.

"I don't get it?" King's girl says.

"She's right, we walked right into a trap." There's my baby. "Bishop!" she shouts, ignoring the other girl's protests and telling her to shush. "I know you're here I can feel the hairs on the back of my neck standing up and there is only one person in this fucking world that gives me that reaction." My chest expands with the first full breath I have taken in weeks knowing she hasn't stopped loving me. "Come out, you fucking pussy!" she screams.

"Now!" Bishop shouts.

Chapter Twenty-Five

Carlina

The sudden brightness from the lights blinds me for a moment and I have to slam them closed to adjust. It takes two seconds before I snap them open again and freeze. The gun hangs limply in my hand as I stare at the five of them standing in the middle of the room that has tables, chairs, computers, papers and whiteboards scattered everywhere. I feel the three girls slide up beside me but my focus is on the tall, dark and stunningly handsome man in the middle of my brothers. His espresso-colored eyes bore into mine. My heart beats wildly inside my chest at the sight of him... no bruises cover his face, from what I can see, and he doesn't look... battered? He looks fresh and clean, but how?

Bishop cuts a glance to his fiancée and narrows his eyes. His face is blank of all emotion but I know there is no way he would ever harm Kiara. He loves her too fucking much to ever think of hurting her.

"Babe——" Kiara clamps her mouth closed when Bishop cocks a condescending brow at her.

"What did you think you were going to find here?" Bishop's tone is laced with triumph that he caught us red handed.

"I was hoping you would be far away and we could ya know, snatch and grab before you ever found out?" Kiara sounds like a dumbass but she knows exactly what she is doing. She's trying to play innocent so Bishop doesn't take her punishment out on her orgasms as she put it. Both Bishop's brows raise. Knight's face is filled with laughter as he looks at Koby. King's eyes are dark but not in anger... eww that is gross. Gage and Vin stand side by side with unreadable expressions on their faces.

"You broke into my office, stole my keys and followed directions from Gage to free *my* prisoner?" I roll my eyes and answer before Kiara can.

"He isn't your fucking prisoner, he's mine! So hand him the fuck over, Bishop, because I'm done with your shit." My breaths are coming in short rapid pants, I've never womaned up to my brother like this before but I meant what I said. I'm done with this family and the bullshit that comes with it. A dark look enters Bishop's eyes and a dark smirk graces his face. I'm not the only one who notices that something is going on with him because Kiara whispers an *oh shit* beside me.

"He was free to go two days after we brought him here. He has his freedom, Carlina." My heart stops in my chest. I begin to feel hot and tears start to build behind my eyes as I shake my head denying what he is saying. "Ask him." I look to Vin who has a guilty look in his eyes. For weeks I thought I was dying because I couldn't save him. I pictured him hurt and bound to a chair being tortured daily, yet he's been free and he never came for... me. A sharp pang hits me in the chest when realization dawns on me. Vin used me to get to my brothers. I turn ready to walk away so they can't see me cry when he finally speaks.

"Gucci, wait!" Like the lovesick fool I am, I stop in my tracks, keeping my back to him unable to look at him.

"Let her go," Bishop snaps.

"Fuck you. This is between me and your sister." I hear him come closer and will him silently to not come any closer, he doesn't. "Gucci, look at me, please." The broken tone of his voice is the only reason I give in and slowly turn to face him. He stands in the middle of the room with my brothers at his back, it's then I notice he only stopped coming for me because Koby and Kiara stepped forward ready to stop him. His eyes implore me to listen but my heart is broken and I don't think I can hear him admit to me that I was just a pawn to be played.

"If you hurt her, I will gut you myself and send pieces of you back to your father. But, I'll keep your fingers to hang from the mobile I'll hang over my kid's crib so they know what happens to people who hurt the ones I care for." Vin's face scrunches in disgust. Knight begins to laugh behind him and wink at his girl... Koby is one badass that I am glad is on my side.

"I never wanted to hurt her—" I cut Vin off ,unable to stand here and listen to his lies.

"But you did! You've been here the whole fucking time, Vincent. I've been dying inside daily picturing the horrors you must have been going through at the hands of my own brother." He at least has the decency to look sheepish. "I fucking begged him to tell me where you were. I-I begged all of them to help me find you and this whole time you've been here doing... what?" I'm shouting now, feeling the remnants of my tears flowing down my cheeks, but ignore them. Vin darts his tongue out to moisten his lips and shoves his hands in his pockets.

"I've been working with them," he says softly. Movement out of the corner of my eye catches my attention and that's when I spot Luka, Mav and other guys that work for my family slowly coming out of a room in the back. I focus back on Vin and disgust rolls through me.

"So, that was the plan, huh?" His forehead creases in confusion. "You seduce me, get me to fall for you and hey, why not fuck me as well while you waited for your in with my brother?" King, Knight and Bishop both mutter beneath their breaths but I ignore them, they aren't stupid enough to believe we weren't sleeping together. Vincent's eyes widen in horror, he takes another forward but the girls block him again, earning a growl from him.

"I never fucking used you, Gucci. I told you I would never lie to you ever. I have kept true to my word—"

"Bullshit!" I scream. Vin moves until he is standing in front of Kiara and Koby.

"Move," he growls.

"Not happening," Kiara grits out.

"Touch either of them and the deal is off," Bishop snaps. I look to my brother and that's when I see it in his eyes. He made a deal with Vincent and that's why he's here willingly. I shake my head in disgust that my own brother could do this to me. I look back to Vincent. As a sob breaks free, his face crumbles in pain at the sight of me.

"You made a deal with my brother?" I hiccup, he nods his head which just causes my tears to flow faster.

"I had to," he says softly.

"Was any of it real to you? Did you even care or love me for a second?" He growls and pushes past both girls. The guys shout behind him but he ignores them as he cups my face between his hands. His touch feels like a balm to my battered heart. Just the feeling of him touching me makes me feel like I can breathe again, that he will keep the night mares away and keep me safe from the monsters of my past that haunt me nightly. He bends at the knees so we are eye level, his eyes flick between mine searching for what, I have no idea.

"Every second was real. I do love you more than anything. I had to make this deal, Carlina. I didn't have a choice." I pull free of his hold, his face falls but he allows me to put space between us.

"What deal?" He stands there quietly for a second pondering how to answer me but Bishop answers before he can.

"He agreed to help us take his father and Pauly down, if I gave him the one thing he wanted most in this world."

Devastation consumes me but I make sure to keep my face blank. He's right, he never lied to me, he always said his end game was finding his sister and saving her. A part of me hates him for it but another part of me understands and respects his loyalty to his blood. It's just going to take me a long time to convince my heart he made the right choice.

Chapter Twenty-Six

Vincent

I grind my teeth in anger, the fucker worded it like that on purpose to keep her away from me. I can see the utter heartbreak in her eyes. I open my mouth to set her straight and tell her the whole truth but she beats me to it.

"I get it, I really do." I shake my head, no you don't, baby. "I hope you find Selena. I wish you both well, Vincent, I do." Again, I open my mouth to speak but she steps sideways until she can see her brothers. "I'm not staying here. You can try and stop me but I'll never stop leaving. I cannot sleep in that fucking room one more night!"

"We'll change your room," Bishop says. He's a fucking

fool. He doesn't understand that it isn't just the room. The whole fucking house brings up bad memories for her because of what happened in that house.

"No, I don't want to go back to that house, I can't. You won, B. You got the help you needed to win your war but it cost you your sister." I hear his footsteps pounding toward us as he moves to stand beside me, keeping his eyes on my girl.

"I'm doing this for all of us, Carlina. Everything I have done is because of all of you, I had no choice—"

"You always have a choice, Bishop!" she screams.

"Everyone get the fuck out now!" King shouts. Everyone except for the nine of us stay where we are.

"I didn't, Carlina. I never wanted this fucking title or to run shit!" My brow furrows as I turn to peer at Bishop.

"Bullshit, you did it for yourself so you could go after Kiara!" Tears stream down her cheeks like a broken faucet. I want to wrap my arms around my girl but she needs to do this on her own.

"I did it for *you*!" Bishop roars. I feel the others creep in closer to us, Carlina's eyes round to the size of dinner plates.

"Bullshit—" Bishop cuts her off.

"You want the truth?" he growls as he stares down at his sister who nods stiffly.

"Fuck," King curses beneath his breath from my other side.

"The guy you're fucking should have been your step son." Carlina's mouth hangs open. I sway on my feet as I look from him to her in fucking horror. "I wanted Tony dead but knew it would start a war like the one we are in now. I wanted to watch him bleed for hurting the girl I've been in love with since I was a teenager, but the final fucking straw was when I found out he was marrying you off to Vinny Murelo." Carlina stands there silently shaking, she's gone pale and looks like she might be sick. Bishop eliminates the space between them, bends so they are at eye level as he places his hands on her shoulders. "I killed Tony to save you, Carlina. I let you and the twins draw your own conclusions because I didn't want you to know what he had planned for you. King only found out after the fact when I had no choice but to tell him. I thought Vincent was here to take you to his father and fulfill Tony's final deal. I see now... I was wrong." I stare at the back of his head taken back by his words.

"You... killed him for me?" she whispers brokenly.

"Yeah, Car. I told you I would never let anyone else hurt you and I meant it. I will never let anyone touch you again, Carlina. I swear on my fucking life I will try to make up for not protecting you when you were younger every day until the day I'm six feet deep in the earth." A sob tears from her as she smacks his hands away and launches herself at him. They hold each other tight and close. My girl cries into her brother's chest as he slowly turns them to meet my gaze. His eyes are rimmed red, I can tell that moment he just shared with her was something fucking hard for him. I nod showing him my respect for telling her the truth. She needed that, she needed to know that her brother would do anything for her and she wasn't alone. I walk toward them until there is a foot of space between me and them. I hold Bishop's gaze not daring to back down because I will fight if I have to in order to keep my girl. "You do this, you help me and my family and I will give you *both*." My eyes widen and a lump forms in my throat as Bishop pushes back from Car, places a kiss to her forehead and steps away.

"I know you know I'm behind you, Gucci." She still refuses to face me, fine. "I never gave you up, Carlina. I couldn't." She slowly turns to face me, trying to hide the hope in her gaze but fails. I reach out and grip her face lowering my face to hers. I take a moment to just breathe her in. I stare into her eyes as I tell her the whole truth. "I did make a deal, he promised to give me the thing I want most in this world." A broken smile graces her stunning face.

"You deserve to find your sister, Vin—" I cut her off because she doesn't get it.

"The thing I want most in this world is you, Gucci. I made a deal with your brother so you wouldn't have to choose between me or them. I love you, Carlina, and there will never be another that could compare to you. Your brother just promised to help me find her as well."

"You chose... me?" I smile at my beautifully broken girl and my heart fucking soars, knowing I get to keep her forever and there is nothing anyone can do about it.

"I'll always choose you, baby. You come second to none." She smashes her lips to mine and I moan into her mouth. She wraps her arms around my neck as mine grip her waist. I deepen the kiss needing more—.

"That's enough!" We break apart but keep our bodies flush against each other and turn our heads to see the three girls and Gage hiding their smiles, while the other three shoot death glares my way. "Never and I mean fucking never again do I ever want to see that shit!" Knight growls. He pins his sister with a glare of warning, which just causes her to laugh. Fuck, I didn't realize how much I missed the sound of her laugh until now.

We pull up to her family home, I feel her tense beside me in the backseat. I grip her hand in mine and give a squeeze, letting her know I'm right here. King puts the car in park and we all file out. Knight pulls up behind us a second later and they all climb from their car as we stand here and wait. I know this is a test, Bishop allowing me into his sanctuary is him showing me that he is trying without using words. I understand his hatred toward me now, I had no idea about the deal Vinny had struck with Tony about Carlina. The thought of my girl being near my father or him ever laying his fucking disgusting hands on her makes my stomach roll. I'll kill the son of a bitch before he ever gets within ten feet of her.

"Knight, take the girls inside and show them where to... go." Knight wraps his arm around Koby's shoulders and makes his way toward the house. Allison places a kiss to King's cheek before following after them. Kiara shoots Bishop a wink as she moves past him but she stops in front of me with a look of determination on her face. I flick my eyes to Bishop who just looks up at the sky muttering something beneath his breath.

"Okay, you got the warning from the guys but now it's my turn." Carlina buries her face into my side, her body shakes with laughter. "It's always going to be chicks before dicks."

"Princess—"

"Shut up, Bishop. You got your turn, now it's mine." My brows jump to my hairline and I fight to keep the smirk from my face. "He may have the guns and all the men but I have the fucking claws and believe me, Vincent Murelo, you hurt my girl and I will claw your fucking eyes out." She nods to herself and turns to leave but stops and peers over her shoulder. "Also, I know you have houses everywhere.

You want to win brownie points with me, you can start by giving me my own room at your mansion in Aspen."

"What the fuck, Kiara?" Bishop snarls. She shrugs her shoulders and smiles at her man.

"I need somewhere to run away to when you piss me off." She quickly scurries away before he can snap at her. It takes a lot for me to not laugh. My girl slowly pulls out of my hold, the nervous and unsure look in her eyes makes me feel like an ass for staying away from her.

"I swear, I'll find you as soon as I'm done." She nods.

"Okay," she whispers as she turns to follow after the others.

"He'll be in the guest room and not yours!" King shouts. Carlina pauses and turns to pin her brother with a look that would make a weaker man quiver.

"Unless you want to hear me screaming his name all night long while I come all over his co—"

"Shut the fuck up and get inside!" Bishop screams with disgust written all over his face. A shudder rolls through him which just causes me to curl over and laugh. "I ever hear that fucking shit and I will cut your cock off, fucker," he grits out as he shoulders past me.

Chapter Twenty-Seven

Carlina

"Are you sure? I know you hate being in there as much as me?" Kiara hauls me against her, wrapping me in a hug. I return her embrace and relish in this moment with my best friend.

"I did hate that house, part of me always will I guess, but I've also made some of the happiest memories of my life in there with Bish. As long as I have him, I'll be fine." I pull back and smile gratefully at my bestie. We both sniff and try to fight the tears then break out into fits of laughter. She grips my hand and leads me to the small living room in the pool house where Ally and Koby sit. Knight was here but Koby kicked him out saying that we needed to talk about girl things. He argued until she finally admitted that they wanted details on my sex life. My brother went as white as a sheet and scurried from the room like his ass was on fire.

"Okay, spill I want every detail, that man is like a tall glass of brandy that I want to swallow whole." Ally, Kiara and I all laugh at Koby who just sits there unashamed with a smile on her beautiful face. I love watching her with Knight. He's changed so much and I know it's all thanks to this blonde bombshell who is pregnant with the future Murdoch. I fill them in on everything from the day I met him to the day I was brought back here.

"You joined the mile high club?" Kiara shrieks. I clamp my hand over her mouth to quieten her down, which causes us all to laugh. Ally popped a bottle of wine that was in the fridge while I was telling them everything and I admit, I have a bit of a buzz going. Koby doesn't seem to mind that she isn't able to drink and I love that she isn't salty that we all are.

"It was incredible, honest to God, Vincent's tongue was blessed by the gods but his dick—" I stop speaking when Allison splutters and spits some of her wine out. Koby pats her on the back with a weird look on her face. I look to Kiara hoping she can fill me in on what's wrong with Ally but her gaze is fixated on the door. I swallow loudly and slowly turn to peer over my shoulder and cringe. Bishop stands there fuming, King looks sick, Knight is glaring at Koby and then finally I look to Vin who is staring right at me, smirking. I smile sheepishly.

"Blessed by the gods, huh?" I cringe and duck my head, while the girls laugh. I can't believe Vincent and my brother's heard that. "Come on, Gucci, I wanna hear the rest of the story." I cover my face with my hands to hide my embarrassment.

"Jesus Christ, don't fucking answer that, Carlina." I peek through my fingers at Kiara who rolls her eyes and stands.

"Bishop, calm down."

"That's my sister!" B protests.

"And that's her man. The girl is gonna get dicked, you have to accept that." My hands drop to my lap. Kiara shoots me a wink as she strides toward my brother, grips his hand and begins to lead him from the room. She peers over shoulder and says to me, "All those descriptions have me wanting to try them out—" Bishop clamps a hand over her mouth, wraps his arm around her waist and carries her from the room while we all laugh. Koby and Ally both stand next, Knight rushes over to help Koby and it's endearing to see how much he loves her. Ally moves to her man and King wraps his arms around her placing a kiss to the top of her head. I never thought there would come a day where my brothers found their other halves. They are rough and deadly but around their girls they are calm, peaceful... they found their homes in these girls.

"See you in the morning, Car?" I nod and wave to Ally and smile my thanks.

"It's good to see you smile." I smile wide at King and my heart warms when his eyes soften.

"See you fuckers later. I'm going to fuck Koby until I pass out." My face contorts at Knight's brazen words. Koby rolls her eyes and leads him out the door, mumbling about her being the one fucking him. The door closes, then it's just me and Vin. I nibble on my lip, suddenly nervous to be alone with him. I can feel his heated gaze on me but I can't look at him. I hear the soft footfall as he makes his way to me. He stops when my shoulder brushes his chest. I take a deep breath and turn to look at him and gasp when I see the burning need in his eyes.

"Vin—"

"I need inside you, Gucci, now." I clench my thighs together.

"But—" He grips the back of my neck, silencing me.

"No buts. I'll tell you everything you want to know *after* I fuck you." I dart my tongue out to moisten my lips, his eyes tracking my movement and a small groan tumbling from his lips, causing the ache at my center to grow.

"Okay," I manage to say before his lips are crashing against mine. It's a messy kiss, our teeth clash as we fight for control. We tear the clothes from our bodies until we both stand here in our underwear. I can see how hard he is through his plain black boxers. Vin moans when he runs his gaze over the red lace bra and thong set I'm wearing. Before I can open my mouth to speak, he's on me again, shoving his tongue in my mouth then gripping the backs of my thighs and lifting me. I wrap my legs around his waist and cup his face between my hands, not willing to break the kiss for even a second. He moves blindly through the house, opens the first door and growls in my mouth when he realizes it's the bathroom. "Last door at the end," I mumble into his mouth. Vin eats up the distance with his long strides and kicks the door closed behind us.

I grind down onto his cock and relish in the pained hiss that escapes him. Good, he deserves to be teased and tortured for a bit after leaving me wondering if he was alive for weeks. His hands grip the globes of my ass, squeezing. I grind down onto his cock again ready to keep teasing him until he grips my waists, breaks our kiss and holds my gaze as he says,

"I fucking love you, Gucci." Then he throws me. I

squeal in surprise as I sail through the air. I land on the bed and bounce twice before he is leaping on top of me, nudging my legs apart so he can settle himself between them. His eyes burn with lust as he stares down at my tits, then leans back on his haunches, grips the clasp in the middle of my chest and unclips it. The bra pops open and drops to my sides allowing my tits to be free. My nipples are hard and aching for him to touch them or fucking taste them. I can feel how fucking wet I am and I swear if he doesn't start touching me soon, I'm going to combust. He grips the sides of my thong and slowly peels it down my legs, then balls the material in his hand, and brings it to his nose and moans. "Fuck, I love the smell of your cunt."

His words have heat burning through my body, my need for him growing by the second. My clit is aching to be touched, my core clenching on nothing but air begging for him to fill me with his cock. He leans down and captures my right nipple between his teeth and scrapes them along it. I arch off the bed and cry out, then moaning when he flicks his tongue across my nipple and sucks it into his mouth. The feeling of his warm, wet mouth on me has me bucking my hips trying to find some sort of friction to alleviate this ache he's causing. He switches to my other nipple, drawing a long, loud cry from me. It's been too long since I have felt his hands, mouth and tongue on me, even longer since his cock has been buried inside me, joining us as one.

"Vincent, please, I need you inside me, now!" I beg. I don't care right now, I need to feel him inside me more then I need to take my next breath. His eyes darken as he shuffles off the bed, pushes his boxers down and his cock springs free. It's red and looks angry as fuck that he hasn't seen the inside of my pussy for a month. I clench my thighs together but Vin grips my ankles yanking me to the edge of the bed.

My ass is balancing on the side, he pushes my legs up to my head and that's when I feel his cock prodding at my entrance. I tense in anticipation, ready and willing for him to shatter my body and rock my world.

"I can't go slow, baby." I meet his hooded gaze and pin him with a firm look.

"I don't want slow. Fuck me hard and deep, then make love to me later." My words are his undoing. Vincent slams his cock inside me and we both cry out. He's so deep inside me that I can feel every twitch he makes. He slowly blinks his eyes open, then begins to move inside me.

"Fuck, Gucci, your pussy is clenching the fuck out of me." I reach up and grip his arms making sure to dig my nails in. A hiss escapes him, his eyes lighting up with pure and utter hunger.

"Make me come!" Three little words is all it takes for him to fuck me like a starved man. My feet are on either side of my head, at this angle I feel like his cock is in my throat. His thrusts are measured and sure, each one hitting that perfect spot making me hot with need. I feel my orgasm build with each thrust. "Vin..."

"I know," is all he says before he picks his speed up and slams harder inside me twice more before I'm screaming his name and seeing fucking stars. He pulls out of me and my legs drop limply either side of him as aftershocks wrack my body. I watch in a lust filled haze as he grips his cock and pumps himself six times before he throws his head back roaring my name. Spurts of his cum land over my stomach and tits... and fuck if the sight of him getting himself off to me isn't the hottest thing I have ever seen. He drops his hold on his dick and flops forward, capturing my lips in a searing kiss. I moan, ready to go again but he pulls back and stares down into my eyes. "Your brother said every man in this world has to mark what's theirs and I just marked what's mine." A shiver rolls down my spine. I never thought I would be the type of girl that wanted to be *marked* or kept but fuck, I want Vincent to mark every single part of me as his, because he is *mine*.

"I love you." His eyes soften as he places a chaste kiss to my lips and slips from the bed offering me his hand. I take it without hesitation. Once I'm on my feet in front of him, he smiles cockily.

"I love you too, Gucci. Now, let's shower and clean me off you so I can do it again." I laugh but lead the way to the ensuite none the less.

Chapter Twenty-Eight

Vincent

Carlina and I are the last to arrive at breakfast. Bishop and King pin me with a look of disgust but I ignore it. Everyone in this room knows why we were late and I give zero fucks. My girl was insatiable and needed to be sated, how could I deny her? We fucked on every surface of that pool house and finally passed out as the sun started to rise. We got an hour tops of sleep before I had my face buried between her thighs waking her with an orgasm. She of course had to return the favor and swallowed every fucking drop of me. I'm not a selfish lover, so of course I had to fuck her to make sure she came again. We showered, only to wind up fucking in there again before we finally emerged for some much needed carbs to refuel.

"Well, well look what the *pussy* cat dragged in." I fight my smile as I claim the seat next to Carlina, who shoots Kiara a withering look. Kiara just laughs and ignores Bishop's burning glare into the side of her head.

"Hi." I slowly lift my gaze to the opposite side of the table to find a beautiful little girl with bright eyes staring back at me. I look to the right of her to find Ally smiling at me encouragingly.

"Hi?" I rasp out. Ally chuckles lightly before placing a kiss to the top of the girl's head and making the introductions.

"Vin, meet Mela. Meelz, baby, this is Vin." Ah, this is King's daughter. I can feel his heated stare on me but I keep my focus on the little girl who is too pretty to be related to that ugly fucking father of hers.

"You pretty," she says. I choke on my spit as the girls all swoon. I clear my throat and smile wide.

"Nah, you're way prettier and thank goodness you take after your momma because you're beautiful." King snorts and mutters beneath his breath. I cut a glance to Ally who is hiding her smile behind her coffee cup and wink.

"Eat, then my office in twenty." Bishop pins me with a look as he adds, "Don't be late."

I help the girls pack away and clean up after breakfast. The four of them stare at me like I'm a strange fucking being which just confuses the fuck out of me. Finally, having enough of the stares and whispers, I turn away from the sink and ask,

"What?" The four of them exchanged loaded looks before Ally speaks up.

"It's just—" Kiara cuts her off, clearly wanting to get straight to the point.

"None of the guys help clean up. They eat and run and here you are actually helping and washing dishes! It's a fucking weird sight to see." I cock my head to the side, slightly confused.

"Uh... I feel like that's a loaded statement that I shouldn't answer?" Carlina bites her bottom lip to keep from smiling. The other three stare at me with a strange look on their faces.

"This blows," Koby quips as she rolls her eyes.

"I've never seen King even rinse his own coffee cup!" Just as Allison says that, Gage, King, Knight and Bishop storm into the room with angry looks on their faces. Bishop looks from me then to the girls before settling his gaze back on me.

"I said don't be fucking late!" I throw my hands into the air in frustration.

"I was helping clean up the fucking mess!" I snap in annoyance. "Unlike you lot..." I make sure to run my gaze over the four of them with pure disdain in my gaze as I speak. "I didn't and still don't have a fucking maid to clean up after me. If someone fucking cooks you a meal the least you can do is clean up to show your appreciation!" The four of them eye me like I've lost my fucking mind.

"Well said," Ally chimes in.

"Hell yeah, bang on the money, Vinny boy," Kiara says, earning a scowl from Bishop.

"What the fuck did we just walk into?" Knight tries to whisper but fails miserably.

"A fucking trap, we walked right into a trap they set for

us," King replies. I roll my eyes at the idiots and go back to washing the dishes. A second later I feel someone slide up beside me. I turn my head to see Gage standing there with a dish towel in his hand ready to help out.

"I never had a maid, nanny or anyone to pick up after me. Don't judge me when you don't know me. I cook, clean, work and maintain my own home without the help of anyone, remember that next time you want to hurl accusations around." Something in me eases at his words. Gage isn't like the other three. He had a rough upbringing and appreciates the little things in life unlike his brothers.

"Sorry, my ma raised me to help out and always clean up. I'm not used to... this." I pass Gage a plate as he snorts out a laugh and shakes his head.

"Yeah, me either bro." The two of us continue to wash and dry the dishes until the last fork is clean. Once we're done, I wipe down the counter and turn to find the three Murdoch brothers sitting at the breakfast bar glaring at us. I cut a look to Gage who looks just as confused as I do. I look to the far wall where the four girls are leaning with their arms crossed over their chests. "Uh, what's going on?" Gage and I were so lost in conversation that we didn't even listen to a thing any of them were saying behind us but clearly, we missed something... big.

"You should have shot him in the fucking head," Knight snarls while shooting me a dark look. I dart my gaze to Carlina and quirk a brow. She smiles as she pushes off the wall, saunters over to me looking like a goddess and doesn't stop until she is in front of me. She places her hands on my chest and reaches up on her tiptoes. I bend down to help her out. She places a quick kiss to my lips before she stands back and places her hands on her hips.

"The girls and I thought it would be a good lesson for

the *boys* to watch how real men act." The three *boys* in question snicker but are quickly silenced when the girls move to stand behind each of their guys.

"Gucci, you're not exactly earning me any points here with your brothers. We were raised differently, that's all," I say low enough only her and Gage are able to hear me. Her eyes soften as she gazes up at me.

"You don't need their approval, you have mine and that's all that matters." Now that has me getting hard. I will my cock to be good. The last fucking thing I need right now is to get hard while her whole family is looking at us.

Chapter Twenty-Nine

Carlina

We all follow Bishop into his office, the girls and I refused to be left out. Well, except for Allison who went to check on Mela. Bishop takes his seat behind the desk. Kiara tries to sit on one of the other seats until he clears his throat. Rolling her eyes, she makes her way to him and drops down onto his lap. King takes one of the seats in front of Bish's desk, Gage sits next to him while Vin, Knight, Koby and I claim the couch. Knight settles Koby onto his lap. Vin pulls me down onto his lap, wraps his arms around my middle and buries his face in the crook of my neck.

"Luka got word that Pauly received the shipment last night via land—" Koby cuts Bishop off.

"How? I'm monitoring all his movements and have been watching his compound around the clock." Koby is pissed, but it's not directed at anyone. She's angry at herself for letting them past her.

"I set the shipment up. We plan to make a move on them before dawn tomorrow. I want this shit over with. Everything is in place and ready to go. Vincent bought us a twenty-minute window to get in. Vin found a way to get a truck into the compound where Pauly and his father are hiding out." I peer over my shoulder to meet Vincent's gaze, He smiles reassuringly but I can't fight the feeling of dread that is working its way through me.

"What's in the shipment you sent?" Koby asks. My brothers all smirk knowingly, but Bish cuts Vin a look silently telling him to answer, which he does.

"The truck is rigged with C4 and set up to remote detonate. We get in, take the kill shots and leave before the truck blows the place up." I furrow my brow confused.

"I thought you wanted the men he had?" I ask Bishop. The smirk is gone and his expression changes to annoyance.

"Those guys are too loyal to their Dons, we'll find another way—"

"I'll ask Tony," Kiara cuts in. Bishop sighs but even he has to know that Tony Bennett is the best option he has.

"No." Everyone turns to Vincent, taken back by his outburst.

"Why?" King demands.

"Because, you cannot bring a hoard of men into Russia without them knowing about it. The best thing to do is get your plant in and wait for them to be able to infiltrate their organization. They have people in the government, police, army, hospitals, you name it, they have it. Vladimir runs Russia, there is no doubt about that. To take him down you need to be smart and patient."

"And how do you suppose we do that, Vincent?" I'm surprised that Bishop isn't being an ass and brushing Vin off.

"Gage needs to find a way in. He needs to weed out the rats and find a way to turn them all against Vlad," Vin answers as I look to Gage. He is going to go undercover in the Bratva, he could get killed!

"How?" Knight asks. Vin looks to Knight and Koby with a devilish smile on his face.

"You both are going to help me remotely hack every server that they have. Vladimir has to have dirt stored somewhere and I'm betting all the information we need is stored behind a fuck load of encryptions that we will need to decipher."

"And how are we supposed to get a *keylogger* into his hard drive?" Koby snaps.

"*We* don't, I do." I'm on my feet in a nanosecond and glaring down at Vincent. He at least has the balls to look bad that he didn't tell me this. "Gucci—"

"Don't you dare fucking *Gucci* me! When the hell were you going to tell me you were going to Russia?"

"While you were orgasming?" The girls chuckle, while the guys snicker. I narrow my eyes to slits, a whoosh of air escapes Vin before he speaks again. "Carlina, you know what my job is, what it entails and what I have to do. I'm fucking good at what I do and I've never missed a shot before until... you." He climbs to his feet ignoring everyone else as he cups my face between his hands and implores me with his eyes to understand. "I'm leaving with Gage. I'll be back as soon as I plant the bug, then I'll work remote."

"From where?" I whisper.

"Here," Bishop answers for Vin. Warmth spreads through me that Bish isn't being an ass about this whole situation. I reach up and grip Vincent's forearms, holding his gaze so he can see how fucking serious I am.

"You better fucking come back or I swear I'll burn each of your houses to the ground and spit on your fucking grave." A wide smile spreads across his face before he quickly plants a kiss on my lips.

"Deal, Gucci."

"King!" At the sound of Allison's worried shout, everyone is on their feet and racing from the room with King leading us.

"Allison?" King screams, I can hear the panic in his voice.

"In here!" she calls back. We all come barreling around the corner into the living room. King rushes to Allison who is standing behind the couch looking pale as fuck. He grips her face whilst running his gaze over her, checking for any injuries. She bats his hands away and turns to the TV mounted on the wall, she lifts her hand that holds the remote and turns the volume up.

'Yes, that's right, Cameron. Local authorities are now at the scene and we can confirm that a body has been pulled from the water. A local fishermen spotted the body early this morning on his way back to shore and alerted local police. We have no identification at this time—'

"Turn it off!" Knight shouts. Allison fumbles with the remote for a second before the TV goes black. No one speaks, everyone is too lost in their own heads trying to come to terms with what we just saw. Vin's arms wrap around my waist as he pulls me to him, I can feel his warmth against my back but I still feel so... cold. My baby brother, my beautiful innocent baby brother who would never hurt anyone is...

"Boss?" I turn to see Luka standing in the entryway. Bishop's gaze is still on the blank screen, standing still as a statue, unblinking. I don't even know if he's breathing. "Boss?" Luka tries to draw his attention again but gets nothing. "Bishop!" Luka yells, and that finally snaps him out of it. He shakes his head and blinks rapidly before looking around the room. King holds a sobbing Ally to his chest, his eyes are void of any emotion. Koby has her arms around Knight who is as pale as Ally was. His eyes are rimmed with tears and I can see the devastation in his eyes. Kiara hugs Bishop around the waist resting her head on his chest, but it's like Bishop doesn't even feel her there, his arms hanging limply at his sides.

"What?" Bish croaks out. Luka moves into the room and stops in the middle so we can all see him. I can tell from the look on his face that he already knows what we saw.

"The body was dumped this morning. Someone looped my video feed so I wouldn't pick it up until the news crew announced it."

"Why?" I breathe. Luka flicks his gaze to me and the pity in his eyes has me leaning further into Vin.

"Someone outside of the families is doing this. I don't have proof but I'm working on it. Someone knows where we go, what we do, where we are at any given time and they are playing in my blind spots." The frustration is clear in Luka's voice, he hates being outsmarted.

"Whoever is doing that to you is more than likely the one who hired me to take out Carlina." Luka nods his agreement to Vin. "We find out who hired me to kill her, then we find your rat."

"We don't have a fucking rat!" King growls.

"Yeah, you do, it's someone in your close circle," Vin argues.

"How would you know?" Bishop asks.

"Someone knew Carlina ran from you or was planning to. They knew what time she was leaving and where she was going. They know Luka is watching every camera throughout the city and Koby and Knight are hacking every server for details about Rook. They know all your blind spots because they have been briefed on them, by you!" I hate to admit it, but Vincent is right. I startle when Gage speaks, I forgot he was even here.

"It's Mav." Everyone stares at Gage like he has lost his damn mind, but then it clicks, the video Vin showed me of the meet with the Dons. Mav was there.

"I trust him," Bishop snaps.

"Then you're a fool. I've been trailing Mav since Kiara got here. The dude always seems to have the right intel at the right time and can never explain how he got it. He's a fucking rat, Bishop!" Gage shouts. Bish opens his mouth to fight back no doubt, but I cut in before they can get into it.

"Gage is right. Vin was keeping tabs on his father and watching him. He showed me a video of the families meeting together and Mav was there. I saw him, Bishop."

"I knew he looked familiar when I saw him at the warehouse," Vin mutters behind me.

"The night at the docks, he was there and never did a thing when Ivan was gonna shoot me before Rook jumped in the way to save me," Koby speaks quietly as if everything is starting to fall into place for her.

"Where the fuck is Mav?" Bishop demands.

"I haven't seen him, boss. He went to do a run this morning to collect the drops but I haven't seen him since," Luka answers.

"Find him." Bishop's eyes burn with unfiltered hate. When he finds Mav, he is going to pay slowly for what he has done. He could have saved my fucking brother! "I want him alive, Luka. Get Mike and Carlos down to the morgue. I want them with that body until a formal ID has been made. Our plans remain the same. We move out tonight and take out the last two, then Gage leaves in three days for Russia." Luka nods and turns to leave but stops when Knight speaks.

"*If* it's... him, you call me, Luka. Not Bishop or King, you fucking call me!" Luka slowly turns to face Knight and gives him a stiff nod. "If anyone touches... the body, I want to know about it. No one is going to cut him open until I see, clear?"

"Yeah, I got you, Knight. I'll have men stationed at every exit until a formal ID has been made." Luka's words seem to relax Knight slightly, in a sick fucked up way I think it's a good thing that Bishop isn't changing his plans. This way it will keep Knight distracted until we find out if it is... Rook.

Chapter Thirty

Vincent

Leaving Carlina tonight was one of the hardest things I have ever had to do. I know she needed me especially finding out they may have found her brother's body. She told me to go and be useful and make sure her brothers all made it home safely, but I know those words were for my benefit not hers. We still have another hour to go before we reach Washington D.C where Pauly's safe house is. Luka drives while King rides shotgun. Bishop and I are in the middle seats with Knight and Gage in the back. Bishop refused to allow anyone else with us, he said he can't trust anyone now. No one has been able to find Mav, he must have been alerted somehow and chose to run. The question I keep asking myself though is, there is no way Mav could work for the families if he was the rat. He has to be in with the Russians to know about all the shit he does.

The tension in the car is so thick you could cut it with a knife. No one has said a word since we left the house. We all know we may be good at what we do, but no matter how good you are, there is always a chance you won't be coming home breathing. Bishop briefed everyone on what he wanted when this job was done. He wants Knight to continue running the old Ramano territory and King to keep running the Romello territory. He hasn't decided what he wants to do with the Polizzi and Murelo territory yet, but even he knows he has to have someone running it or another will try and take over. I had thought he would put Gage in charge of one of them but with him going to Russia that wouldn't be the best idea.

"Luka." The sound of Bishop's voice pulls me from my thoughts.

"Yeah, boss?"

"You'll run the Polizzi territory until Gage is back." The sudden intake of breath behind me lets me know that this declaration is a shock to Gage. Bishop turns to look over the seat at Gage, he keeps his face blank of all emotions as he speaks. "Once you have dealt with the Bratva, you will take over from Luka and run things there."

"I... Uh, I don't know what to say," Gage mutters.

"Say you won't fuck it up and then we're good."

"I won't fuck it up, Bishop. You have my word." I can hear the conviction in Gage's voice and I have no doubt he will do well in his new position. "What about the Murelo territory?" Bishop shifts his gaze to me and I tense. I flick my gaze to his and wait.

"Carlina will run it." My eyes widen in shock. "I wanted each of my brothers to take over and grant my sister her wish of freedom from this life, but I can no longer do that. Car will take over and that way a Murdoch will sit at the head of all parts of New York and no one will be able to challenge us. My family will be free of threats and no one will be able to fuck with us." I nod my understanding but ask.

"And when your sister is no longer a Murdoch, what then?"

"*Oh shit,*" I hear Gage mutter from the back, but ignore him as I keep my eyes on Bishop.

"She will always be a Murdoch at heart and that is all that matters." I shake my head, he is so dense.

"There is no way in fucking hell that my girl will be running a fucking territory where her life will be in danger daily because of how high she is ranked." Bishop opens his mouth but I push on needing to get this out. They all need to hear this and know where I stand where she is concerned. "I love your sister and I *am* going to marry her, whether you like it or not. Carlina belongs with me and I will fucking fight each of you daily for the rest of my life if it means she is with me. It's because I love her and want a family with her that I am telling you now. *No,* she will not be running things for you. I won't allow her to put her life on the line daily out of some sort of sense of duty to her family." Bishop rolls his lips over his teeth and cocks his head to the side studying me for a moment. I can feel the other three staring at me but I don't dare look away from the Don.

"I don't like you." I smirk which just earns me a glare from Bishop. "I hate that my sister is with you, I don't support it at all." I shrug not really giving a fuck what he thinks. "But, I do support the fact that you love her enough to risk your life to help us. I know you don't like us or even care for us. You being here right now shows me what my sister means to you. Help us win this fight and then go after the Bratva and I'll reconsider Carlina's position as the head of her territory." I smile wide and shake my head.

"That wasn't a negotiation, Bishop, that was a promise. Carlina isn't going to run shit and if you force my hand we'll disappear and I guarantee you, no hacker will find us. If you don't believe me just think back to when you couldn't find her for months while she was with me in Brazil." His jaw is locked as he tries to tame his anger. "Don't force my hand. If it is something she wants to do for herself and not because you demanded it, I'll stand by her side and keep her safe every fucking day of my life."

***

We all have our night vision googles on and are strapped with vests, helmets and ear pieces. I'm packing heat all over my body and have my blades strapped to each thigh. I lift my Barrett M82 sniper. It's fitted with a silencer and the perfect gun for what I need. I scope out the area making sure that there is a clear path for Bishop and his men to get through. King is leading the other half with Gage around the other side where they have another sniper set up. I'm the best long-distance shooter they have. It fucking pains me that I'm not down there with them but I promised my girl I would bring her brothers home and I'm no liar.

"Vincent, you set?" The hushed whisper of Bishop's voice come through the ear piece.

"Hold five, I got three to the right and two moving east," I answer as I line my shot up.

"Can." *Bang.* "You." *Bang.* "Take." *Bang.* "Out?"

"Done, head right I'll clear the path but stick close to the house." And I do, every time I see someone not with us they get a hole to the head. I spy movement on the top of the house and make quick work of taking out two of the guards up there, what I don't fucking expect is for one of them to fall from the roof. "We've been made, take cover!" I shout through the earpiece. I ready myself for the onslaught of men that will be coming, and chuck my night vision off before I get blinded when they switch on the lights. Not two seconds later we are bathed in bright lights and shots ring out. Bishop's men scatter, no point in hiding now they already know we're here. I keep Knight and Bishop in my sight and take out anyone who gets close to them making sure they have an unobscured path to their target. Once they disappear inside the house there is nothing I can do but wait and hope they make it out.

I spot Gage and King running toward where Bishop and Knight went inside, I take out the two guards in front of them and keep dropping guys until they are inside the house. Minutes tick by and still no sign of them, I try to contact them through the ear piece. When I get no response for the third time, I say fuck it and make my way down the bank. I don't slow my pace as I pull my gun and drop anyone who gets in my way. With the amount of fucking money they must pay these guys, the least they could do would be teach them to fucking shoot!

I race through the house and come to a stop in the entryway. I look left and right but see no one. I creep further into the house to try listen for any sounds of a fight, that's when I hear a cry for help. I take off down the hall and skid to a stop in front of an open door that leads to the basement. I keep my gun ready and in front of me as I slowly creep down the stairs.

"You're going to pay for this!" The sound of Vinny Murelo's voice sends a cold shiver of dread through me. I make sure to keep to the shadows as much as I can and stay silent. I reach the bottom stair and peek around the corner. Fuck! Vinny has a gun pointed at Bishop's head, King is being held back by two guards, Knight is on his knees with Pauly holding a gun at his temple. I look around but don't spot Gage. I turn the other way and decide to check out what else is down here and to make sure no one can ambush me from behind. I curse silently beneath my breath when I find a body sprawled out on the floor, I know it's Gage. I kneel down beside him and check for a pulse, a sigh of relief escapes me when I feel one. I shake him a few times to wake his ass up, his eyes slowly blink open and he opens his mouth but I cover it with my free hand shaking my head. He nods, I stand and help him to his feet while giving him one of my other guns and a knife.

"They have four," I whisper, Gage nods and follows behind me. I spot another entry point to where the others are being held and motion for Gage to go that way. At least then we will have covered their only exit.

"Say goodbye to the other twin, hope he finds the bitch we dumped!" Pauly taunts, he cocks his gun back and I nod to Gage as we burst into the room with our guns trained on both Vinny and Pauly.

"Drop the fucking guns!" I shout. Pauly fucked up and took a step away from Knight dropping his gun slightly. Gage took the opportunity and put him down. The two guards holding King shove him forward so they can draw their weapons. Knight grabs Pauly's gun and jumps to his feet. Vinny keeps his gun on Bishop as he stares at me, I can see the shock in his eyes at seeing me alive.

"You're dead," the fucker whispers, earning a smirk from me. "You good for nothing bastard I should have sold you not your sister—" I don't even let him finish, drawing my gun faster than he can blink and put a hole right in the center of his forehead. Two more shots ring out alerting me to the fact Knight and Gage took care of the guards. I watch as Vinny draws his last breath and crumbles to the floor like the sack of shit he is. I move forward and spit on the disgusting cunt that I shared DNA with.

"I'll find Selena and I'll bring her home," I say to his corpse. I don't wait for the others as I head out to end this fucking fight. I can feel Bishop's gaze burning a hole in the back of my head as I leave the basement.

Chapter Thirty-One

Vincent

I don't bother to turn back and watch the fireworks as Bishop pushes the detonator. A split-second passes before the loud boom sounds out behind us. I rest my head against the glass and close my eyes. I thought after all this, finally getting my revenge would make me feel... better but it doesn't. If anything, I feel like more of a failure now than I did before. I could have kept him alive and pulled the whereabouts of my sister from him. I should have done something but my anger and hatred took over and I snapped.

"He wouldn't have told you the truth." I open my eyes and look to Bishop, but I don't bother to move my head or speak.

"What?" Bishop scrubs a hand down his face and that's

when I notice he isn't wearing a suit for once, he's in a black tee and black cargo pants. His tattoos are on full display, I hadn't taken any notice earlier but the guy is covered in ink.

"He would have told you what you wanted to hear just to stay alive. Vinny has no idea where your sister is." I scowl at the fucker.

"And you do?" I grit out.

"I'll answer that if you do something for me?" I eye him warily for a beat before nodding. "Work for me, Vincent. Do what you do best for me and I'll get you your sister but trust me, you might not want to disturb her life."

"What the fuck is that supposed to mean?" I snarl, a sad smile graces his face.

"Your sister was what, around eight and you were about ten when your father... sold her?" I grind my teeth so hard I think they may snap but manage to nod. "Koby found her records and Luka managed to find her whereabouts now." I sit up straight and turn to face him, he has my full attention now.

"Where is she?" I demand.

"She lives in Romania with her husband and three children. Selena Murelo is now Selena Albu. She is twenty-nine years old and has been married for eight years to the police officer who rescued her from a... house when she was seventeen. She is now a spokesperson who helps women heal after being trafficked and she runs at least four women's shelters. Your sister is happy, Vincent. I swear to you, I had no fucking idea she even existed. I have never and will never deal in the skin trade. I am trying to do better. I may deal with drugs, guns, casino's and all the other shit but I have never dealt with selling people." When I feel something wet slide down my cheek I reach up and catch it with my finger. I'm crying? Bishop says nothing as he sits there and waits for me to process what he has just told me. Selena is alive, she's happy and has a family of her own... a husband who loves her. That is all I ever wanted for her was to be happy, I want to bring her home with me but that would be selfish, all seeing me would do is bring back the memories of her own father selling her.

"You just gave up your only leverage to get me to work with you?" Bishop doesn't comment on the fact I changed the subject, I appreciate that.

"Actually, I'm hoping you will just agree to work with us. You didn't have to save me or my brother's tonight. You could have run but you didn't, and that right there goes a long way in my books." I nod, unsure what the fuck to say to be honest. "There's something else, it's about Russia..." He clamps his mouth closed and pins me with a weird look when I laugh.

"You, King and Knight aren't staying back, are you?" He rolls his eyes clearly annoyed that I figured out his plan.

"No," he grits out. I shake my head. He is going to get his dick ripped off by his girl when she finds out.

"What do you want from me?" I ask.

"I need somewhere safe for the girls—"

"Done, they can have my house in Aspen. I sent Marco there to lay low. He can keep watch over them—"

"I don't know this fucker," Knight pipes in from the back. I pin him with a look that says don't fuck with me.

"Marco is my cousin and he is the reason why we got in tonight. He helped me find the dirt on all of my enemies. He would die before he ever let any harm come to those girls." I mean every word I say, I trust Marco even though he was pissed about me not killing Carlina. He sees now what she means to me and has since apologized. King turns in the front seat to face me, pinning me with a dirty look.

"My daughter will be there," he growls.

"How about I fly Marco out here, you meet him and everyone can travel back together?" I suggest. None of them are happy with the idea but they don't have much other choice. Bishop may not like me but he trusts me to keep Carlina safe. "My house in Aspen is set with motion detection all around the woods. The alarm system is top of the line, the whole thirty acres is fenced and electric. The house has panic mode and will lock down in two point five seconds. That house is the safest place for them to be. If Marco being there is too unsettling for you three, then I will send him to my apartment in Ibiza until I get back."

Three days later...

Bishop holds Kiara tightly against him, Knight has Koby wrapped around him, King and Allison stand in an awkward three-way hug with their daughter as I stand here with my girl hugged to my chest and her arms wrapped around me while I bury my nose in the crook of her neck and breath in her scent. Kiara, Allison and Koby didn't take the news well that their men would be coming with us. Koby threatened to castrate Knight, Kiara said she would shoot Bishop but Ally, she burst into tears and begged King not to leave her and their daughter. I spy Luka out of the corner of my eye and know it's time. Him and eight others of Bishop's most trusted will fly with the girls to Aspen.

Marco didn't want to cause any trouble so he took my offer to fly to Ibiza until I return. Tony, Kiara's father, has agreed to give Bishop the man power he needs when the time comes. The morgue is running dental records on the body and we won't have an ID until that's done. The body is unrecognizable Bishop told us. He was the only one who went to the morgue. There has still been no sign of Mav. No one has seen or heard a word from him, which just tells us all that he was the rat. Koby has been trying almost daily to get in contact with Anya but had no luck. We can all see the worry in her eyes for her friend and the guilt she feels. Anya saved Koby and her brother and now Koby is determined to return the favor.

"I don't want to let go," my girl whispers as her grip on me tightens. I nip at her neck and relish in the shiver that rolls through her. Neither of us slept a wink last night as I couldn't get enough of her. Every time I thought of leaving her, my hunger for her would come back and I was inside her again in seconds.

"I don't either, baby, but I have to do this," I say quietly. I hate that I don't have a time frame on when I'll be back. Gage said he can be inside the Bratva within a week and build up from there, but I need to get inside their building and not get caught. I don't tell her any of that though.

"Promise me if things get bad, you'll leave. Promise me you'll come back to me, Vincent, because I can't lose you... I won't survive that." A sob tears from her and it fucking destroys me to see her cry. I hold her tighter and place kisses to the top of her head. Bishop catches my eye and nods indicating it's time. I take a deep breath and slowly untangle myself as I take a step back, her eyes are red and puffy from crying. I gently wipe away her tears and lean down to kiss her. I pour all of my love for her into this kiss, hoping she knows without me saying that she is my world. I will fight with my dying breath to get back to her. Pulling back, I rest my forehead against hers.

"I love you, Gucci. Just think about it like you're going

on a girls trip and I'm... going away to bond with your brothers." She snorts out a laugh and that brings a smile to my face. She searches my eyes for a few seconds before kissing me. I try to deepen it but she pulls back and turns, walking away from me without a backward glance as she follows the girls and Luka to their plane. A lump begins to form in my throat as I watch my heart walk away from me. I only look away when the captain lifts the stairs of their private jet and closes the door before he flies away.

"If we don't make it back, I'm gonna be fucking pissed." I nod my agreement. "My girl finds out in four weeks what we're having and it sucks I won't be there for that scan, but I am not missing the birth of my kids. You fuckers hear me? You have eighteen weeks tops to get in and end this or I'm out." I can't argue. If I was in Knight's position, I would be saying the same thing.

"Come on, we need to get to our plane." We all ignore Gage and don't move until the girl's plane is in the air. We're flying out of a private airfield a few miles out of town, flying under the radar so we don't alert the Bratva we're coming. It's only the five of us going, Bishop has left Luka to run everything while he is away. He is only to make contact if it is an absolute emergency. None of us can make contact with the girls in case we are being followed. From the moment we board this plane we will all be radio silent. We are literally flying into enemy territory and for the first time since I started working for the agency over a decade ago, I'm worried. I have a sinking feeling not all of us are going to make it back alive.

Epilogue

Gage

Six weeks...

I manage to keep my word and get into the Bratva as a foot soldier. I'm stuck guarding the outside of the club they operate in, never getting a glimpse inside. I haven't even laid eyes on the Pakhan himself, only a couple of his captains, one of them being the fucker that shot my brother. The morgue's result came back no match. Bishop and King have given up hope that Rook is alive but Knight hasn't and neither have I. To give up hope means to give up on Rook and that is something I can't do... I will never give up on my family. Bishop and I may not see eye to eye all the time but he is blood. I would die for my brothers and sister in a heart-beat. The crackle of my radio pulls me from my thoughts. I wait with bated breath, hoping by some fucking miracle that I manage to get some information or a chance to see Vlad.

"We got a situation out back, go clean it." I grind my teeth to keep from telling the Russian fucker to suck my dick. Their English is so fucking bad you can barely understand the fuckers. I've been studying Russian and learning to speak it since I first found out about them going against my family. I need to be able to understand what they are saying if we are going to end this. We've managed to pinpoint who most of the politicians are that work for Vlad thanks to Knight and Vin hacking their bank records and finding large sums deposited into their accounts. "Hurry up!"

"I'm nearly there," I growl, I'm so fucking over this shit. I'm not the type of guy who can sit behind a desk like Bishop or play on a laptop all day like Knight. Fucked if I know what King does. Vin and I are the same, we're hands on guys and like to settle things that way. I slam to a stop when I reach the back of the club. The base from the music is louder around this side. I look around the poorly lit alley that holds the dumpsters but see nothing, I'm about to radio back when a figure shifts out of the shadows. I draw my gun and aim at the person's head, waiting for them to make a move into the light so I can see their face.

"I'm not here to fight."

"You're American?" And a girl but I don't say that out loud.

"No, I'm Russian and I don't have a lot of time before they notice I'm missing." The hairs on the back of my neck raise, my senses go into overdrive as the threat of danger becomes apparent.

"Who are you?" My voice is firm and leaves no room for argument.

"It doesn't matter, all you need to know is that he leaves the country for business in Ukraine in four days. The only guards will be the four you work with and yourself at the house––"

"I only work at the club," I interject. I can't see her but I can picture her shaking her head.

"No, you will be moved to the house to make sure no one leaves." I lower my gun and straighten up as I stuff it back into my waistband.

"I don't understand what the hell you are saying?" I growl in frustration.

"Bring your computer man, he can get inside and find what he needs while you stand guard." I freeze but make sure to keep my shock from showing.

"I don't know what the hell––"

"I know everything, Gage Sanders, don't take me for a fool. You have four days to prepare your brothers and computer man, you won't get another chance like this."

"Who the hell are you and why should I believe you?" Anger laces each of my words. She finally steps into the light and fuck me, she is beautiful. Her blonde shoulder length hair looks almost white. She has piercing blue eyes that remind me of the sky, wearing a blue, sequined dress that hugs her curves in all the right places. And her legs, they are so long and the perfect length to wrap around my waist.

"If he ever found out I was here speaking with you, he would kill me." She moves forward until there is a small amount of space left between us and hands me an envelope, her eyes bore into mine. "If you tell anyone, even your brother's about the contents of that envelope, I'll make sure you never find it." With that said she turns to leave, going back toward the shadows but I call out stopping her.

"Tell me your name," I demand, her shoulders sag slightly before she composes herself and holds her head high, while continuing to walk back into the shadows. Before her silhouette can disappear from sight, she says, so low I would have missed it if I hadn't been paying such close attention to her,

"My name is Anya Volkov."

Oh, fuck!

I shake out of it and quickly head back around the front to my position. I'm on high alert now and can feel the tension radiating through my body. I just met the daughter of the Pakhan and she just gave me a way into his home. Can I trust her? I ponder over that thought as I discreetly open the envelope she gave me. It's a polaroid picture, I flip it over and everything inside me freezes, my heart skips a beat and everything begins to get hazy as I stare down at the picture in my hand. Chained like a dog to the wall, naked and bruised looking so malnourished and dejected. Blood and dirt caked all over, chunks of hair missing, eyes that once seemed so bright and full of life are filled with nothing but pain. I stuff the photo in my pocket and make a vow, Anya Volkov will fucking pay for this stunt even if it's the last fucking thing I do!

Click the link to read gage's story,

Turned By The Pawn

THANK YOU!

Are you still with me?

Do you hate me a little bit?

I want to say I'm sorry but I also don't want to lie, don't worry you won't have to wait long for Gage's book, I promise.

How badass was Car? Did she not learn to hold her own and stick up for herself? Want to know a secret, I wasn't going to write a book for Carlina but then Vincent popped into my head and wouldn't quit till I wrote his story and boy I'm so glad I did.

I love these two so freaking much and I'm glad they found their happily ever after with each other.

Thank you so much for reading Tempted By The Queen, if you would leave a review on **Amazon, Bookbub** or **Goodreads**, it would mean a lot to hear your feedback.

Gage's book is **<u>Turned By The Pawn</u>!**

Mafia Romance

Murdoch Mafia Series

Played By The Bishop

Tormented By The King

Tortured By The Knight

Tempted By The Queen

Turned By The Pawn

Ruined By The Rook

Murdoch Mafia Novella

Stalemate

Memento Mori Series

Reign Of Royal

Broken By Sin

In Havoc Lays Chaos

Godfathers of the night

London has Fallen

Damned By His Angel

Re Della Strada

Shattered Soul

Fractured Heart

Tainted Essence

Fairytales With A Twist

Condemned Beast

Secret Society/ Bully

Filthy Few

Forever Filthy

Filthiest Of Them All

Masked Men Novella (Pure Smut)

Dirty Priest

Dirty Daddy

Sports Romance

<u>Playing For Keeps</u>

Offside

Touchdown

End Game

Hail Mary

Blindside

RH Sports

Hate Us Like You Mean It

MM

Love Me Like You Mean It

Paranormal Romance

<u>The Veil Of Obsidian</u>

Of Time And Carnage

<u>Curse Of Fate</u>

Dream

Fate

Nightmare

Redemption

Anarchy

<u>Brutal Savages</u>

Savage Lies

Brutal Truth

Savage Beast

Brutal Beauty

ACKNOWLEDGMENTS

Baby daddy, husband, my nightly dick ride...what can I say aside from I love you and thank you for all that you do for me. You're my best friend and I love you.

Tash, my girl! Thank you so much for loving each of these character's like I do and helping me with all the things you do.

Clare, the best beta reader out, thank you so much for loving all of my books and boosting my ego daily, I appreciate you so much.

Lizz, my amazing and bomb asf editor, thank you. You make these books what they are and I cannot thank you enough for that.

My mum, bless you for giving me life mummy. I am so grateful to you for that, you support me no matter what I do and I love you more then you will ever know for that. The boss man, daddy, I love you old boy and wouldn't be who I am today without you pushing me to never settle. Thanks dad, I love you.

My ARC and street team, thank you all so freaking much for all your support, love and dedication to each of my books. You ladies are truly amazing and I cannot thank each of you enough.

Last, but not least, my amazing readers, thank you so much for reading my books and falling in love with each of the guys and girls. Without your support and love of these books I wouldn't be able to live out my dream of being a full time author so, thank you.

Sam Xxx

ABOUT THE AUTHOR

Samantha Barrett is a dark romance, PNR author who loves to write out-of-the-box stories. She is originally from the land of the long white cloud, New Zealand. She is totally fluking her way through this whole author gig, if she isn't writing you can find her kicking back with her kids and husband with a bag of chips and a glass of wine in her hand. Sam loves Twilight and is a TWIHARD proudly.